YEARS
of pure reading pleasure

100 Reasons to Celebrate

We invite you to join us in celebrating
Mills & Boon's centenary. Gerald Mills and
Charles Boon founded Mills & Boon Limited
in 1908 and opened offices in London's Covent
Garden. Since then, Mills & Boon has become
a hallmark for romantic fiction, recognised
around the world.

We're proud of our 100 years of publishing
excellence, which wouldn't have been achieved
without the loyalty and enthusiasm of our
authors and readers.

Thank you!

Each month throughout the year there will
be something new and exciting to mark the
centenary, so watch for your favourite authors,
captivating new stories, special limited
edition collections…and more!

Dear Reader

This book is a very special one for me for two reasons. Firstly, the book's setting is very close to my heart—it's set in a fictional house in Norfolk, and part of the book takes place in Norwich, my home city. I've had several books published on the city's history—it's one of my great passions!—and that leads me to the second reason why the book's special to me: Mills & Boon is 100 years old this year, and I'm so proud to be part of that history with my 30th book for Mills & Boon. (Though, if you're counting—because of the way the publishing programmes work, this is my 29th on the shelves.)

History really matters to me, and this whole book is about the importance of history—and also when it's time to stop depending on the past and start looking forward to the future. It's about confronting fears and knowing when to trust someone.

Add a gorgeous hero, music, cake, best friends who know you better than you know yourself, and you can see why Alicia's life changes for the better.

I hope you enjoy your journey into my favourite part of the world. I'm always delighted to hear from readers, so do come and visit me at www.katehardy.com

With love

Kate Hardy

SOLD TO THE HIGHEST BIDDER

BY
KATE HARDY

◉ᵀᴹ MILLS & BOON®
Pure reading pleasure

First published in Great Britain 2008
Harlequin Mills & Boon Limited,
Eton House, 18-24 Paradise Road, Richmond, Surrey TW9 1SR

© Kate Hardy 2008

ISBN: 978 0 263 86372 7

Set in Times Roman 10¼ on 12 pt
171-0308-51326

Printed and bound in Spain
by Litografia Rosés, S.A., Barcelona

Kate Hardy lives on the outskirts of Norwich with her husband, two small children, a dog—and too many books to count! She wrote her first book at age six, when her parents gave her a typewriter for her birthday. She had the first of a series of sexy romances published at twenty-five, and swapped a job in marketing communications for freelance health journalism when her son was born, so she could spend more time with him. She's wanted to write for Harlequin Mills & Boon since she was twelve—and when she was pregnant with her daughter, her husband pointed out that writing Medical™ Romances would be the perfect way to combine her interest in health issues with her love of good stories. Now Kate has ventured into writing books for Modern Heat.

Kate is always delighted to hear from readers—do drop in to her website at www.katehardy.com

Recent titles by this author:

ONE NIGHT, ONE BABY
BREAKFAST AT GIOVANNI'S
IN THE GARDENER'S BED

For Dot—my wonderful agent—with love

CHAPTER ONE

HE WAS half an hour early.

Some people would call it rude. Jack Goddard called it a good opportunity to scope things out properly, make sure there were no hidden catches.

Would Allingford Hall look as good in real life as it had in the brochure? Or had clever photography hidden some kind of eyesore right next door?

So far it looked promising. Norfolk would be the perfect place to chill out. There was so much blossom on the black-thorns and in the cow parsley growing on the verges, it looked as if there had been an unseasonal fall of snow. Jack knew that if he wound his window down, the air would be thick with scent.

Two more bends and, according to his satnav, the narrow opening on the left was the driveway to Allingford. A long drive, flanked with copper beech trees. Better and better: no neighbours meant there would be no complaints about noise.

And when the house finally came into view, he smiled.

Exactly what he'd hoped it would be.

The house was E-shaped with crowfoot gables and angled chimneys; the middle bar of the E was a double-storeyed porch, while the end gables were three-storeyed. The house was perfectly symmetrical; clearly it was the original design rather than having bits added higgledy-piggledy over the years.

This place, he thought, had a history. A heart. And if it turned out to be haunted, so much the better. If the gardens were big enough, it would be the perfect backdrop.

All he needed was the planning permission, and he'd be open for business.

He parked on the gravel in front of the house, and as he got out of the car a yellow Labrador came bounding over to greet him. Although the dog's bark was muffled by the teddy bear it was carrying, the sound was clearly loud enough to have alerted the woman who came rushing behind the dog. A woman dressed in jeans and a T-shirt that had both seen better days, teamed with elderly tennis shoes. Her hair, the colour of winter wheat, was pulled back in a scrunchie. And there was a smudge of dirt across her cheek.

He blinked.

In his world, women wore power suits and high heels, with immaculate and fashionable coiffures—not to mention make-up. This woman didn't look as if she was wearing so much as a slick of lipstick; and although her eyelashes were thick and dark they didn't look caked in mascara.

What you saw was exactly what you got.

And he *wanted*. The sheer desire that flooded through him actually made him sway slightly towards her.

He couldn't remember the last time he'd felt like that about anyone. Including Erica.

He really hadn't expected this today.

'Jack Goddard?' she asked.

Her voice was gorgeous. Low-pitched but not over-quiet. Cultured. In control.

He found himself wondering what she'd sound like when

she'd lost control. When she was so turned on that she couldn't see straight…

He pulled himself together. Just. 'Yes.'

She wiped her hand on the back of her jeans and held it out towards him. 'Sorry about the dirt. I was expecting you a bit later.' Not quite a rebuke: there was nothing snide about her tone. Not quite an apology, either: more like, This is me—like it or lump it. 'Alicia Beresford.'

She was the owner of the house? He'd been expecting…well, someone posh. A battle-axe or a princess. This woman was neither. She was well spoken but she didn't have that snooty air that most of the Hons he knew had. She was slightly scruffy and very, very touchable—and suddenly all he could think of was stripping off her grubby clothes and lifting her into the shower. With him.

Ignoring the fine layer of soil that still remained on her palm, he took her outstretched hand and shook it. She had a good handshake, dry and firm, but it felt as if a bolt of lightning had just shot through him when the skin of his palm met hers.

And from the way her eyes widened slightly, it was obviously the same for her.

Oh, hell. He really needed to get himself under control. Number one, he never mixed business and pleasure. Number two, Alicia Beresford didn't seem the type to do flings—and he never did more than a fling, nowadays. Not since Erica.

The dog, clearly not wanting to be left out, dragged the teddy bear across his knees, leaving a muddy smear on his trousers. And although Alicia clearly made an effort to hide her grin, her amusement still showed in her eyes. 'I apologise for my dog's bad manners,' she said. 'We can sponge your trousers in the kitchen. Hopefully it won't leave a mark.'

Sponge. Jack had to close his eyes for a moment to get rid of the mental picture of Alicia Beresford kneeling before him, wielding a sponge against his naked flesh. This really wasn't supposed to be happening. He never let himself get distracted in business. So why on earth was he letting this woman affect him like this?

It wasn't as if he were sex-starved. Quite the opposite.

But it was a long time since he'd last felt a pull this strong towards anyone.

'Think of it as a sort of compliment,' Alicia was saying. 'Saffy doesn't offer to share her teddy with just anyone.'

'Saffy?'

'Short for Saffron.'

'Appropriate for a golden Labrador.'

'Indeed.' She took a deep breath. 'What do you want to see first—inside or out?'

She didn't pussyfoot around, he noticed. Well, from what his dossier said, she couldn't afford to. Not with the amount of tax she owed on the place. Her father had died five years ago and left the place to his son—who'd been bitten by an insect in the rainforest and died of some rare tropical disease four months ago, leaving the place to Alicia. Jack's sources said that her brother had barely paid half the inheritance tax he owed, which meant the whole lot landed on her. A tax bill that equated to her entire salary, before tax, for the next twenty or so years.

Not that he was going to take advantage of it and make her sell the place for a fraction of its worth. In his view, you could do business successfully without having to grind other people into the dust. If the house lived up to its promise, he'd be happy to pay a fair price—the asking price. Especially as he'd get possession very quickly. Now he'd decided to take the sabbatical, he wanted to start his plans as soon as possible. 'As we're outside, we might as well start here,' he said.

There was an avenue of rhododendrons to the side of the house, covered in purple and white and pink and yellow flowers. It opened out into a walled area, which contained neat beds of what was clearly a kitchen garden, plus an old-fashioned greenhouse and a brick building with a glass front.

'That's the orangery,' she said, following his gaze towards the brick building, 'though it hasn't been used as one for a long time.'

Now they were closer, he could see. It was a storage space. There were neatly stacked trays of pots, another wheelbarrow, more garden implements and what looked like a ride-on lawnmower. A very, very posh garden shed. 'So how old is the greenhouse?'

'Early eighteen hundreds,' she told him. 'It's still got the original iron brackets for the roof.' He noticed a flicker in her eyes as she looked at the building. Passion. This was what made Alicia Beresford tick. This was what she really loved. The garden.

She led him through a different gate and another avenue of rhododendrons into a formal garden at the back of the house. He was no expert, but it looked neglected, as if it was too much for whoever was looking after it. There was a wheelbarrow by one border where she'd clearly been working.

So was *she* the gardener he was supposed to keep on? There was no way she could possibly cope with a full-time job as well as taking care of the kitchen garden and this formal garden. It would be too much for anybody.

And then he stopped thinking when he saw the other side of the house.

There was a huge lawn sloping down to the edge of a lake. Teamed with the wide skies of Norfolk, this would be absolutely perfect for what he had in mind. Why on earth hadn't the estate agent put that view into the brochure? It was *stunning*.

He caught his breath. 'That's fabulous.'

'Mmm.' She still sounded cool and poised, but her back was just a little too straight. It told him how much of a wrench this was for her, showing her family home to a prospective purchaser. In her shoes, he'd be pretty upset, too. So he'd try not to make this hard for her. But all the same, as he followed her towards the courtyard at the back of the house he couldn't help glancing back over his shoulder at the lake.

Next was the old stable block. It was a good size and, converted properly, would suit his purposes well. At the moment it appeared to be used as a store, but he could definitely see it in his mind's eye, cleaned up and fitted out.

'And this is the house.' She walked over to the front door, the dog trotting behind her. Her jeans were faded from washing, and he'd bet the denim was soft to the touch. It shocked him just how much he wanted to touch the material, how much he wanted to slide his hand over the curve of her bottom.

Alicia Beresford wasn't fat, but she had feminine curves. Glorious curves. Curves that begged him to mould his palms to them.

And he really ought to start thinking with his brain instead of another part of his anatomy. He needed a clear head before he could make a balanced decision.

Ha. Who was he trying to kid? He'd made the decision practically the moment he'd looked at the particulars of the house, and his instincts were never wrong.

Well, *almost* never.

But he learned from his mistakes. Learned quickly and well.

'I assume you've had the details from the agent,' she said as she opened the front door.

'Yes.' He hadn't bothered bringing them with him, as his memory was near-photographic. One country house with outbuildings, land and contents.

'Good. This is the entrance hall.'

The floor was the polished red Norfolk tiles known as 'pamments', and gave the room a warm feel; the walls were cream, reflecting the light from the two windows. A dog-leg staircase in dark wood led to what was presumably the first floor. Jack was surprised not to see a row of family portraits hanging on the wall, given that Alicia's family had owned the place for near on three hundred years, but, knowing how tactless it would be to ask, he made no comment.

'Living room.' Again, the walls were painted cream, and there were no pictures. Jack had a feeling the paint was recent. And he'd just bet it was to cover up patches from missing artwork. Paintings that had probably been sold after Alicia's father died, to cover part of the death duties. There was oak panelling to one wall of the living room, but three windows looking out across the garden made the room seem bright and airy rather than gloomy. Though the heavy drapes were slightly on the shabby side and the furniture could only be described as 'lived-in'. No wonder she hadn't auctioned it off; it would fetch next to nothing.

'Dining room.' It was like the living room, with less furniture and a chandelier that could really use a professional clean.

'Library.' It was a fairly small room with a desk, a couple of battered leather club chairs, and a wall full of bookshelves that had rather a lot of gaps. Clearly, she'd sold all the volumes that were worth anything to help pay the tax bill.

'Kitchen.'

A really old-fashioned kitchen, with a stone-flagged floor, an Aga, a proper butler's sink, and glass-fronted cupboards, which were clearly very old. Like the living-room furniture, it could do with updating, but any work needed to be done sensitively. He rather liked the feel of the room. He could imagine sitting here to discuss business, drinking coffee and eating home-made cake at the scrubbed wooden table.

'Morning, Miss Alicia.' The girl in the kitchen turned and bobbed a curtsey.

And Jack couldn't help staring. The girl sounded like a maid—even though her accent was suspiciously Mockney—

but she didn't look like a maid, with her dyed black spiky hair, heavy eye make-up and blood-red lipstick. She couldn't be more than her late teens. And, rather than a traditional maid's outfit, she was wearing ripped black jeans and a black T-shirt sporting the logo of an up-and-coming rock band.

'Would you like tea, Miss Alicia? In the drawing room?' she asked.

He glanced at Alicia. Did she *really* have domestic staff? Then again, according to the estate agent and his solicitor, there were some conditions to the sale. Ones which meant keeping on a housekeeper and a gardener. He'd already worked out that Alicia herself was the gardener, but surely this teen punk couldn't possibly be the housekeeper?

Alicia rolled her eyes and introduced them. 'Grace Harvey, Jack Goddard.'

'Good afternoon, Ms Harvey,' he said politely.

She gave him an approving nod at the 'Ms'. 'Everyone calls me Grace.'

Clearly she was trying to live down her name, he thought. She wasn't the sort for pearls and haute couture and kid gloves.

She held out her hand. He took it, and discovered that she had a real bone-cruncher of a grip—clearly warning him that she was no servant to be bullied around, and she'd stand up for Alicia.

He liked that.

Because so far he'd got the impression that Alicia Beresford was very, very alone.

'Good band,' he said, gesturing to Grace's T-shirt. 'I saw them at Glastonbury. The new album takes a couple of listens before you can get into it.'

She frowned. 'It's not out until next month.'

'True, but I've got a review copy in the car. I'll lend it to you, if you like.'

Her frown deepened. 'A review copy? How?'

'My best mate's a music journalist. Perks of the job. And he knows I like the band, so he passed it on to me. Got me a back-stage pass at Glastonbury, too.'

Grace looked suitably impressed. 'Wow.'

'I'd better get you that wet cloth,' Alicia said quietly.

'Ah. You've been Saffy-fied.' Grace raised an eyebrow. 'I'll do it, Lissy.' She rinsed a cloth under the tap, squeezed it out and looked at Jack. 'One cloth in exchange for a listen of that CD?'

He couldn't help smiling at her; he liked her directness. Keeping her on as a housekeeper wasn't going to be a problem. 'Deal.' It was the work of a few seconds to deal with the smeared dirt, and then he handed the cloth back to Grace.

'The laundry room's through there,' Alicia said. 'There's a wine cellar beneath it, but frankly there isn't anything down there.'

Sold too, no doubt, he thought. But he took a peek through the door anyway. It was very much like the kitchen, with fewer cupboards and the addition of a washing machine and tumble-dryer. The door at the far end, he assumed, led down to the cellar.

'I'll show you upstairs,' Alicia said, 'then we'll have coffee in the drawing room.' She smiled at Grace. 'Don't worry, I'll make it. You're going to be late if you don't get a move on.'

Grace glanced at her watch. 'Hell's bells and buckets of blood! Paddy's going to scalp me. I'll just put this lot away— I'll finish them in the morning, Lissy.' She stripped off her rubber gloves and started gathering up the cloths and polish.

'Don't worry about it. Leave it—I'll sort it out.'

'You sure?' Grace gave her a grateful look. 'Thanks. See you tomorrow, Lissy.' She nodded at Jack. 'Mr Goddard.'

She was gone before he had a chance to remind her about the music.

Then Alicia showed him round the rest of the house. Upstairs was the same as downstairs: the walls were pale, the rooms had plenty of light inside, the curtains were shabby, and there were hardly any pictures. And most of the furniture was covered in dustsheets.

'It's pointless heating rooms I don't use,' she said, as if aware of his enquiring glance.

'So is Grace the housekeeper?' he asked.

'Part time. Yes.'

'Why do you want her taken on with the house?'

'Her gran was the housekeeper here for years. And this job—together with her part-time job at the local pub—pays her way through her course at art college.' She smiled. 'Actually, Grace is a good contact. She knows everybody. So when the boiler has a hissy fit, she's got a mate who's a plumber who can come and fix it right then for a fair price instead of making you wait a couple of days and charging you a fortune just to turn up.'

He wasn't surprised about the art course. Or that Grace had a family connection to the place. But he was surprised that Alicia had brought up a problem with the house. 'The boiler's temperamental?'

'And the roof needs work, we spend the summer fending off ants and the autumn fending off mice, and most of the wiring's well over thirty years old and needs replacing,' Alicia said, folding her arms and looking straight at him. 'Just so you know.'

Her eyes were beautiful. A deep cornflower-blue. Right now they were cool. What would they look like when she was hot and bothered?

Concentrate on the house, he reminded himself. 'Aren't you meant to be pointing out all the positive things about the place?'

She shrugged. 'Well, if I can't sell it…'

'…then it'll be sold off at auction, probably for less than the tax you owe,' Jack finished. 'Which will leave you with absolutely nothing.'

'Fair point.' Her face shuttered.

He had no idea what was going on in her head. Hurt? Angry?

Bitter? In her shoes, he'd be absolutely livid at the idea of losing his family home because he didn't have enough money to pay two sets of inheritance tax on the house in the space of five years.

'I'll make some coffee. Or would you prefer tea, Mr Goddard?'

'Call me Jack. And coffee's fine, thanks.'

He noticed that she didn't invite him to use her first name in return. Keeping a distance between them.

Right now, it was obvious that she saw him as the enemy.

She paused by a door at the top of the stairs. 'This was Ted's flat—my brother's. One bedroom, a bathroom, a kitchen and living room. It has its own entrance downstairs—as does my flat. So you could use this as a holiday let, or convert it back into part of the main house.' She looked at him. 'Though I have asked that I can continue to rent *my* flat after the house is sold.'

Well, he wasn't going to live here full time. Once everything was set up and his sabbatical was over, he'd go back to London; and it would be useful to have someone around to keep an eye on the place. 'Not a problem, as far as I'm concerned.'

'Thank you.'

By rights, he ought to check out the flats. Make sure there wasn't any major structural problem. But the way Alicia Beresford was holding herself, her back ramrod straight, this was clearly painful for her. It hadn't been that long since she'd lost her brother. Seeing her brother's rooms, talking about selling his things—that would hurt.

So he wasn't going to insist on it and make this even harder for her. The surveyor's report would tell him anything he needed to know.

'Shall we?' he asked, gesturing to the stairs.

The relief in her face was momentary, and it was quickly masked, but he knew he'd made the right decision.

'So you want to move from London?' she asked.

'For a few months. I'm taking a sabbatical.' She didn't push to know more, but he told her anyway. 'I'm a hedge-fund manager.' Just in case she was worried that his budget would only run to buying the house and not to all the repairs and renovations. Not that it would be any of her business, once the house was sold, but he wanted her to know that Allingford would be in good hands. That he wouldn't neglect the place.

'So you want to unwind in the country.'

'Sort of.' He paused. If she was going to stay here, she'd find out anyway. Might as well tell her now. 'I'm setting up a recording studio.'

She blinked. 'Recording studio?'

'Where artists come to make records,' he explained patiently. 'The stable block will be perfect, once it's converted.'

'I see.'

'And that lake's the perfect backdrop for concerts.'

She couldn't have heard him right.

Jack Goddard was going to turn Allingford into a recording studio and open-air concert venue? And, given that he listened to the same kind of music as Grace and where he'd seen that band… 'You're setting up another Glastonbury?' she asked in near-disbelief.

He spread his hands. 'What's the problem?'

'Do you have any *idea* what kind of damage that's going to do to the grounds? And there's nowhere to park. You can't possibly rip up Dad's rhododendrons for a car park—it was his whole life's work. No way!' She dragged in a breath. 'Forget it. I'm sorry, Mr Goddard. You've had a wasted journey. The house is no longer on the market.'

'I think Her Majesty's Revenue and Customs might have something to say about that.'

'Then I'll talk to them again about the National Trust.' She'd asked them to take the house in lieu of death duties, with the proviso that she could stay on in her flat and oversee the garden restoration. Except the house hadn't been important enough and, with the garden restoration in its earliest stages, there was nothing much to see there, either. Just her father's rhododendrons; and despite the fact they were a world-class collection it wasn't enough. 'I'll do them a ten-year business plan.'

Jack shook his head. 'If they've already said no, they're not likely to change their minds.'

'Then I'll talk to the tax people again. Ask them if they'll let me…' She dragged in a breath. How she'd hate it. But with the alternative being a rock festival that would ruin the grounds, it was the lesser of two evils. 'If they'll let me turn this place into a hotel or conference centre.'

'The amount of money it'd take to get the house up to conference accommodation standard—not to mention meeting all the health and safety regulations—means the place wouldn't even begin to start paying for itself for three or four years,' Jack pointed out. 'And all that time you'll be accruing interest on the debt.'

True. She'd already scoped it out and realised it wouldn't work. And she hated him for being right. Even if he was drop-dead gorgeous. The sort of man who'd draw every single pair of female eyes in a crowded room. Dark hair that was deliberately cut to make him look as if he'd just got out of bed, little creases round his mouth that said he smiled a lot, and the sexiest eyes she'd ever seen. Added to the kind of restless energy that practically crackled from him, the faint shadow of stubble because he hadn't bothered to shave that morning, and the way he was dressed in dark trousers and an open-necked white shirt… He was absolutely edible.

Not that her mouth was going anywhere near him.

And not that she should be thinking in this way about him, either. He was the enemy. The man who wanted to buy the home that had been in her family for three hundred years, and then ruin it. She'd planned to restore the original pleasure gardens, and he wanted to turn the area into a car park or a stage.

Over her dead body.

'Right now,' he said softly, 'I'm your best bet.'

Like hell, he was. 'You'll never get permission from the council,' she warned.

'We'll see.' But he didn't sound in the slightest bit concerned. And there wasn't the tiniest flicker of worry in his blue, blue eyes. Jack Goddard was clearly one of those men who was used to driving his decisions through. Well, he would be. He'd said he was a hedge-fund manager. Meaning that he was a high-flier whose yearly bonus could wipe out all her debts and still leave change. Why hadn't she gone into finance or law or something that could've made her tons of money, instead of following her family tradition and choosing horticulture? Why had she sat in her ivory tower, stupidly thinking she'd always be able to live here and spend her life pottering around the gardens?

'So—the sitting room?' he prompted.

Although she felt like telling him where to go, he was a sort of guest here. And her father would have been appalled at her bad manners. She took a deep breath and opened the door to the sitting room without comment.

He smiled when he saw the piano. 'Baby grand. Nice.' He moved the piano stool out slightly and sat down. As if he owned the place.

As he might well do, shortly, unless she could think of another way to pay the debts.

Maybe she could sell herself.

Wanted: millionaire to marry impoverished heiress to a country house. Must be sensitive, with GSOH.

Except by definition a millionaire businessman would have to be ruthless and single-minded. So he wouldn't be sensitive or have a sense of humour. And as for marrying a millionaire footballer or pop star…well, she was at least ten years too old to be a footballer's wife or a rock chick. Even if she managed to find one who liked older women, she wouldn't be glamorous enough to attract him.

There was no way out.

She was going to have to sell the house to Jack Goddard or someone like him. Allingford would be ruined. And he was going to start the process right now—he'd probably hammer out 'Chopsticks' or something equally awful on the piano.

He glanced over his shoulder at her, and her fears must have been written all over her face, because he grinned and proceeded to play 'Chopsticks'.

Really, really badly.

He had no sense of timing, he was playing the bass and the melody in two different keys, he was fumbling the notes…This was torture.

She was about to beg him to stop when the music changed.

Suddenly he was playing Beethoven. The slow movement from the Pathétique Sonata. One of her favourite pieces of music ever—and his timing was impeccable. He followed it up with a beautiful but notoriously difficult Chopin nocturne. Also note perfect. And he was playing from memory, not from a piano score.

When he'd finished, he gently replaced the lid and swivelled round to face her.

'It needs tuning,' he said.

'I know.' With limited funds, you had to make choices. Essential building repairs or having the piano tuned: she'd gone with her head rather than her heart. Which was why she'd stopped playing. Not that she was going to tell him. She didn't want this man's pity. 'You, um, play very well.'

'Thank you.' His eyes sparkled with amusement. 'You know, you really shouldn't make snap judgements.'

The rebuke was deserved, she knew, but it still stung. Like rubbing salt on the raw patch he'd created when he'd talked about holding rock concerts in the grounds and to hell with the gardens. 'I'll go and make that coffee,' she said, and fled to the sanctuary of the kitchen.

CHAPTER TWO

JACK hadn't meant to hurt her. Just to make the point that Alicia had judged him too quickly and he wasn't the kind of man she'd obviously decided he was—a *nouveau riche* oik who confused money with culture. But if he left it like this, it would be even more awkward when she came back with the coffee. Which wasn't a good idea—not if he wanted to persuade her to keep an eye on the place when he wasn't here.

He needed to work with her in the best interests of Allingford.

In other circumstances, she might have reacted differently towards him. Then again, he would've reacted differently, too. If he'd met her at a party, he would've asked her out for a drink. Dinner. Got to know her.

Gone to bed with her.

Though right now wasn't the best time to think about that. He wasn't going to act on the attraction between them—even though he suspected it was mutual—because he never, ever mixed business and pleasure. He'd seen too many colleagues crash and burn that way.

He headed for the kitchen. The kettle was on and Alicia was shaking ground coffee into a cafetière. 'Is there anything I can do to help?' he asked.

'Thank you, but no.' She took two china mugs and a small jug from a cupboard and a plastic carton of milk from the fridge. 'Milk? Sugar?'

'Neither, thanks. I like my coffee unadulterated.' He smiled at her.

'That's easy, then.' She set the cafetière and the mugs on a tray and put the milk back in the fridge.

'Don't stand on ceremony for me,' he said. 'I don't mind having coffee in the kitchen.'

She shrugged. 'You're the boss.'

'No, I'm not. Well, obviously as you're the part-time gardener I'll be paying your salary, but that's incidental.'

'I'm not the gardener.'

He blinked. 'But when I arrived you were working in the garden.' The dirt on her hands and her face testified to that—though he noticed that she'd washed her hands before making coffee.

She shrugged. 'The garden takes a lot of work, and Bert can't manage it on his own.'

'Who's Bert?'

'He was the head gardener in my grandfather's time,' she explained. 'He should've retired twenty years ago, but he lives in this bungalow with a pocket-handkerchief garden and it just isn't enough to keep him happy. I let him grow what he likes in the greenhouse and the kitchen garden; he gives me some of the vegetables and fruit, but he does whatever he wants with the rest. And he does a bit in the gardens for me. A kind of quid pro quo.' Her face tightened. 'I've tried to pay him.'

He said the words she clearly couldn't force through her lips. 'But you can't afford it any more.'

'Actually, he won't let me.' She looked away. 'But, no, I can't afford *anything* right now because I've got a great big tax bill to pay. Rub it in, why don't you?'

'I'm not trying to rub it in. I'm trying to be practical. So let me get this straight: Bert does some of the garden and you do the rest?'

'Yes.'

Even for two of them, part-time, it was too much. There had probably been a team of gardeners in the house's heyday.

As if she'd guessed his thoughts, she said, 'But that's all irrelevant—if you buy the house you're going to get rid of it all and build a swimming pool shaped like a guitar or something.'

He laughed. 'Hardly.'

'Isn't that what rock stars do? Stay in places, chuck furniture through the windows and drive cars into swimming pools?'

'Not all of them. And actually I'd be pretty annoyed if someone did that. I don't mind partying, but I *do* mind vandalism.'

Suddenly she looked hopeful. 'So you're not going to vandalise Allingford with a festival?'

'Glastonbury isn't the only music festival, you know.'

She scoffed. 'So what are you thinking? Glyndebourne?'

'I'm thinking about single-evening events—some of them rock, some of them classical—with a firework display at the end. Just imagine how starbursts would look reflected in the lake at night.' Surely she could see how amazing it could be? And a place like this shouldn't be kept locked away. It needed to be shared. Let other people enjoy its beauty.

'Why music? Why Allingford?'

'Music, because I like it,' he said simply. 'Allingford, because I want the right backdrop—and that lake is absolutely perfect.'

'And you can afford to buy this house on just a whim?'

He could understand how galling it must be for her, when she couldn't even pay the inheritance tax, but even so the question annoyed him. He hadn't been born into privilege. 'You expect me to apologise for finding something I'm good at, working hard and earning a good salary?'

She flushed and looked away. 'No. I'm sorry.' She sighed. 'It's just that…this is difficult for me.'

The admission couldn't have been that easy, either, and his annoyance faded away. He'd be the same in her shoes. And it'd be hard to keep a lid on the frustration and be pleasant. 'I know,' he said softly. 'I'm not trying to make it any harder for you.'

'I just don't want Allingford to change,' she said. 'That view beyond the lake—it's been like that for hundreds of years and it's perfect.'

He agreed with her. So what was the problem?

'Progress doesn't always mean cramming in hundreds of houses into a tiny field,' she said.

Did she really think he was going to turn the estate into a housing complex or something? He shook his head in disbelief. 'I'm not planning to cram in hundreds of houses on the land.'

'But you're going to rip up my dad's rhododendrons to make a car park.'

'Not necessarily. Do you ever open the garden to the public?'

'No.'

Her face suddenly shuttered. He had a feeling there was more to it than this, but he also had the feeling that now was the wrong time to push. He needed to get Alicia Beresford to trust him before she'd open up to him. But he made a mental note: this discussion wasn't over. Not by a long way.

She poured coffee into his mug. 'I'm sorry, I don't have any biscuits to offer you.'

'Not a problem.' He took a sip of the coffee. 'Thank you. This is good.' Strong and hot and bitter, just how he liked it. Saffy came to sit beside him, dropping the teddy and placing her chin on his knee; automatically, he started stroking the top of her head, and she leaned in closer.

He liked dogs, and the Labrador had clearly picked up on

that. Though he had a feeling that her owner was going to take a lot longer to accept him. If she ever would.

Something shifted inside Alicia as she took in the scene: Jack sitting at the kitchen table, making a fuss of her dog. He looked *right*, here. And she had to admit that Allingford had been neglected over the last few years. Even if she had been able to afford the tax, living here on her own was a waste of the house's potential. It needed to be a family home again. Have children running around, playing hide and seek in the rhododendrons and feeding the ducks on the lake and doing cartwheels on the lawn.

Maybe she should take her best friend's advice. Megan was right: it was time for her to move out. Because suddenly she couldn't bear the idea of seeing Jack Goddard walking round the grounds, an arm wrapped round his wife's shoulders while hers was wrapped round his waist.

Which was *stupid*—for pity's sake, she'd only met the man today. It shouldn't matter to her whether he was single or not. It was none of her business. Yes, he was the most attractive man she had met in a long, long time. But she had no intention of doing anything about that; since Gavin, she'd lost her confidence in her judgement of men. And her common sense told her that getting involved with Jack Goddard would be a huge mistake.

So she didn't sit at the table with him. She remained leaning back against the dresser, sipping her coffee warily and wishing she were a million miles away from here.

He looked narrowly at her, but to her relief he didn't push her to make any further conversation. When he'd finished his coffee, he took his mug over to the sink and rinsed it out. 'Thank you for your hospitality,' he said politely.

'You're welcome.' She couldn't say 'pleasure'—because it wasn't a pleasure, signing her home away. But at least he'd been polite. She was equally polite, and saw him out to his car.

When he closed the car door, the window slid down smoothly and he held a CD case out to her and a business card. 'This is for Grace. Tell her to let me know what she thinks.'

Alicia had almost forgotten that he'd promised Grace some music. If he paid this much attention to detail, thought of other people, maybe this wouldn't be so bad.

Ha. Who was she kidding? Whoever bought the house, it would be bad. It would be the end of life as she knew it. Instead of walking and working in the gardens that had belonged to her family for generations, she'd be a tenant with no rights whatsoever. She'd have no say in whatever he did to the house or the garden. All her dreams—well, they'd never be fulfilled now. And she'd better get used to it.

Her fingers touched his as she took the CD case. It was the lightest contact, but it made her skin tingle. Made treacherous images slide before her eyes—visions of Jack Goddard touching her much more deliberately, stroking her skin while his blue, blue eyes went hot and his mouth parted, promising her even greater pleasure. Visions of Jack lying beside her next to the lake, propped on one elbow and leaning over her. Visions of her own head tipping back, inviting his kiss, offering her throat to him.

'Alicia?'

Oh, no. She really hoped he wasn't a mind-reader. Where those visions had come from, she had no idea, but she really didn't need them. Now or ever. 'Sorry. Just thinking about what I need to do in the garden this afternoon,' she said. Which was true, up to a point: she had been thinking about the garden. And the lake. He didn't need to know the rest of it. 'Thank you for the CD. I'll give it to Grace when I see her next.'

And that was it. A tiny spray of gravel, and he was gone.

Half an hour after Jack left, the post came. Yet another letter from the tax people. There really was no escape. She had to sell. And at least Jack Goddard had looked as if he belonged in the kitchen. Maybe, once he'd spent a few days at Allingford, the house would pull him under its spell and he wouldn't change a thing.

Maybe.

She was weeding the border when the phone rang.

'Ms Beresford? It's Sadie from Norfolk Properties. We've had an offer on the house. For the full asking price.'

'From Jack Goddard?' He could be no more than halfway back to London. He couldn't have made a decision that fast, could he?

'Yes. I would recommend that you accept the offer, Ms Beresford,' the estate agent continued. 'We *could* hold a sealed auction in the hope of getting a higher bid, but in the circumstances…'

She knew. She had no choice. 'Then I accept,' she said tonelessly.

'He wants to complete as quickly as possible.'

'All right. I'll talk to my solicitor.'

But by the time she'd managed to get through, Jack's solicitor had already spoken to hers.

The man didn't waste a second.

And she wasn't sure whether she was more relieved or dismayed by it.

'He's agreed you can rent the flat—' and here the solicitor named an extremely reasonable rent '—and he'll keep the staff on.'

Everything she'd asked for.

Everything she would've done herself, if she'd had enough to pay that tax bill.

And Jack had been more than fair to her. He could've refused to let her stay. He could've said he wanted the flats back as part of the house and he didn't want a tenant.

It gave her hope that maybe she'd be able to persuade him to change his plan about the concerts. That instead she'd be able to talk him into restoring the gardens to how they'd been years ago. And he at least would be able to afford to do it in one season, instead of piecemeal, the way she'd been doing it.

'Thank you,' she said quietly.

'And he wants to move in on Saturday,' the solicitor added.

Saturday?

That was no time at all.

Then again, maybe it would be for the best. Like ripping off a sticking plaster in one go instead of trying to take it slowly. It would hurt like hell—but it would also be over quickly.

'But…there's all the paperwork to sort out. We can't possibly do it that quickly.'

'If we pull out all the stops, we can.'

In Alicia's experience, legal wheels moved very, very slowly indeed. 'What if we don't sort it by Saturday? Will the deal be off?'

'We'll sort it by Saturday,' the solicitor said gently. 'I'm sorry, Alicia. I know this is a wrench for you.'

It felt like the end of the world. Not that she was going to admit to that. 'End of the week it is, then.' She swallowed hard. 'Do I need to come in and sign for things?'

'Yes. Tomorrow at nine?'

Just as well it was out of term time, she thought wryly. The end of the Easter holidays. Next week, she wouldn't have been able to take the time off work. 'Tomorrow at nine,' she said.

She replaced the receiver, then slowly walked around the house. So many memories. So much she'd wanted to do…but she hadn't been able to do it. 'I'm sorry,' she whispered as she walked through the rooms—talking as much to her great-great-great ancestors as to the house. 'I'm sorry I let you down. That I couldn't make it work out.'

And in a few days' time, for the first time in three hundred years, Allingford Hall would no longer belong to the Beresford family.

* * *

'For me?' Grace's eyes widened as she looked at the CD. 'I thought he was just showing off. Oh, man. He actually delivered on his promise. And this is going to be so good.' She hugged Alicia.

'Hey. I'm only the messenger. He wants to know what you think of it.' Alicia handed over the business card.

Grace raised an eyebrow. 'I don't think this one's for me. It's a sneaky way of giving it to you.'

'What?'

'He's a bit too old for me,' Grace explained with a grin. 'Whereas you...you're the same generation.'

'I have no idea how old he is,' Alicia said stiffly.

'Don't be so stuffy. Just look at him. He's definitely a man to do.' Grace looked speculatively at her. 'It'd probably do you good, you know.'

'What?'

'No-strings, hot sex with a gorgeous man. Something to get Gruesome Gavin out of your head. Look, you're thirty-four.'

Alicia lifted her chin. 'Which doesn't mean I'm past it.'

'No, but you act as if you're past it sometimes.'

Alicia had known Grace ever since the teenager was a tiny baby, so she let it pass.

'And from the way he was looking at you yesterday, I think he likes you,' Grace added. 'And the way you were looking at him.'

'I was *not* looking at him.'

Grace scoffed. 'You're female. And he's gorgeous. Of course you looked. And you liked what you saw.'

Alicia refrained from commenting.

'I bet he'd be really good at sex,' Grace continued.

Oh, God. Alicia really, really wished Grace hadn't said that. Because she thought so, too. And her entire body was tingling at the idea of being skin to skin with Jack Goddard.

'He's got a really sexy mouth.'

She'd noticed. And, much as she would've liked that mouth to work its way down her body, it was a complete no-no. Alicia sighed. 'Look, there are all sorts of reasons why it's not going to happen.'

'Such as?'

'For a start, he's going to be my landlord, as of Saturday lunchtime. Not to mention your employer.'

'So?'

'So it'll be embarrassing when it's over. Awkward.'

'A mutual fling? Course it won't. Besides, you've been under a lot of stress lately, and good sex is about the best stress-buster ever.' There was an irrepressible twinkle in Grace's eyes. 'Works for me.'

'I am not going to have sex with Jack Goddard.'

Grace folded her arms and looked at Alicia through narrowed eyelids. 'Are we having a bet on this?'

'No, we are *not*.'

'Because you only bet on sure things.'

Again, that so-sure-of-herself grin. Alicia couldn't remember being that confident at eighteen. She wasn't that confident now—not on a personal level, anyway. Work was different: she knew she was good at that.

'So you can't bet against it,' Grace continued. 'Because you know you're going to do it.'

'Grace, which letter don't you understand out of N and O?'

Grace merely laughed. 'You need a good man. Or, at least you need to *do* a good man. And Jack Goddard ticks all the boxes. Did you see what he was wearing? Black trousers and a white open-neck shirt. Add some knee boots and ruffles and get him just a little bit damp in the lake, and—'

Alicia groaned. 'Stop it. He isn't Mr Darcy.'

'No, he's a lot better than your Darcy fantasy. Because he's not going to be stuck up and snooty. I don't have a clue what you see in Jane Austen. All that repression and self-denial—give me a break!' Grace rolled her eyes. 'Lissy, you have to admit the man's hot. Even his hair looks as if he's just got out of bed after some seriously good sex.'

'He probably paid a fortune for that haircut.'

'Money you would've spent on plants. Yeah, yeah.' Grace flapped a dismissive hand. 'Lissy, just do yourself a favour and have some fun for once.'

'I'm perfectly happy with my life,' Alicia protested.

Grace snorted. 'Excuse me. I've known you my entire life and I've heard all my gran's stories about you, too, so you can't lie to me. You're not happy, Lissy, and it's not just because of the house. Ever since Gavin—'

'I don't want to discuss Gavin.' Alicia cut in.

Grace said something short and extremely rude that described Gavin exactly. 'He wasn't good enough for you. Not by miles. But you're still brooding about him and you need someone to help you get him out of your system.'

'I'm coping.'

'There's a huge difference between coping and living,' Grace said softly. 'And I think a fling with a man like Jack Goddard would be the best thing that's happened to you in years. Hot sex with a gorgeous man and no commitments.'

'It's too complicated. And I don't know anything about him.'

Grace waved the business card at her. 'One passport to the internet. Let's look him up.'

Ten minutes later, Alicia leaned back in the chair. 'Well, there's proof for you. For a start, he's younger than me.'

'Six years isn't much.' Grace gave her the cheekiest grin. 'Not at your advanced age.'

Alicia couldn't help laughing. 'You make me sound like an old crone!'

'Because you're acting like one. Anyone would think you're older than my gran, the way you talk.'

Alicia chose to ignore that comments. 'How many different women did we just see on his arm? All gorgeous?'

'You're just as gorgeous—probably more so than they are,' Grace said. 'If you'd let me do something with your hair and then me and Megan—' Alicia's best friend since she was eighteen '—could do something with your awful clothes…'

'*My* awful clothes?' Alicia gestured at Grace's outfit.

'I'll have you know, these are trendy. Besides, I'm eighteen, I'm at art college and I'm doing the teenage rebellion bit. You're way too old for that excuse.'

Nothing ever abashed Grace, Alicia thought ruefully.

Worse, since Grace had done some work experience with Megan's interior design firm, the two women got on well. And Alicia knew the two of them had been plotting to find her a partner; so far, she'd managed to resist their casual suggestions of making up dinner parties, but they were growing more persistent.

'Stop avoiding the subject,' Grace said. 'The point is, you're every bit as good as the women Jack Goddard dates. And he obviously doesn't do commitment. So you can have fun and it's not going to end up in a mess with him expecting to marry you.'

'It's still not going to happen.'

'We'll see,' Grace said, and tapped the side of her nose.

CHAPTER THREE

THE rest of the week sped by. Alicia spent it going through Ted's things and the attic—with the help of Megan and Grace, because this was something she really didn't want to do on her own and she had to admit she needed the help of her two closest friends. By the end of the week they had packed up boxes of clothes and household equipment for charity shops; a couple of bags of documents to shred; boxes of books to go to the university to offer to his colleagues and students; and black bin liners filled with things that were only fit for the dump.

The only things Alicia kept were the watch their father had given Ted for his twenty-first birthday, and Ted's journals from his expeditions. Eventually she'd think about talking to a publisher or storing them in the record office, where everyone else would be able to see his beautiful drawings and students would be able to use them for research, but for now she wanted them close. The last things she had of her family.

That, and a book that really belonged with the house, but she couldn't bear to part with it. Not yet. Sure, she could make a colour photocopy, but it wouldn't be the same.

'I still think you'd be better off moving out,' Megan said. 'Start again, somewhere else. Living here's like rubbing salt in the wound every time you look out of the window or open the front door.'

They'd had this conversation before. And Alicia's position hadn't changed. 'No way. I've lived here since I was two days old. It's my home.'

'But it isn't *yours* any more,' Megan said gently. 'And it's going to kill you, living with that knowledge. With the money you get from the house, once you've paid the tax bill, you'll have enough to get a small cottage with a huge garden. Somewhere you can make yours.'

'I'm hardly going to find and buy a cottage between now and Saturday,' Alicia said.

'Well, no,' Megan admitted. 'But you know you can stay with us while you're looking for somewhere. We've got plenty of room.'

No, they hadn't. And the last thing Megan needed was a houseguest during the last tiring weeks of pregnancy and the first few weeks with a new baby. Alicia couldn't possibly take up the offer, even though she knew it was meant sincerely. 'Thanks.' Alicia hugged her warmly. 'I really appreciate it. But I'll be absolutely fine here.' And she hoped Megan couldn't see her fingers crossed behind her back.

And then it was Saturday.

The day when Alicia had to hand over the house.

At precisely midday, the doorbell went.

Knowing that this would be the last time she opened the front door of her family home, she took a deep breath. 'We can do this,' she told Saffy.

Well, she had to.

There wasn't any other choice.

She opened the front door and stepped outside, followed by her dog. This time, Jack was dressed completely casually, in a black T-shirt, faded jeans and running shoes. And he looked even more gorgeous than he had in that crisp white shirt.

Her mouth went dry.

This was a complication she didn't need.

Keep your mind on business, she reminded herself. And forget what Meg and Grace think. You are *not* having a fling with this man.

'Hello,' he said softly.

'Mr Goddard.' She nodded in acknowledgement—no way would she risk shaking his hand again—and gave him the box file she'd prepared. 'One inventory, as promised to your solicitor. And three sets of house keys, including the ones to Ted's flat. They're all marked.'

'Thank you.' His eyes were kind as he looked at her. 'I know today's tough for you.'

She couldn't answer that. It hurt too much.

Then she realised that there was only one car parked outside. Jack's shiny red convertible. No van full of furniture, no friends to help him move stuff, no family. He was completely alone.

Even though she was pretty sure he was single, given the pictures she'd seen on the internet—and not all men lied like Gavin—she couldn't stop herself asking, 'What about your wife and children? Aren't they coming?'

He raised an eyebrow. 'I told you before about snap judgements. No wife, no children.' He paused and looked her straight in the eye. 'And no girlfriend.'

She felt her face flame. 'I wasn't fishing.'

A corner of his mouth quirked. 'Of course not.'

'I *wasn't*.'

'Will it be a problem for your boyfriend?'

'What?'

'Me living here with you.'

For a second a picture flashed into her mind: the four-poster bed in the master bedroom, with crumpled sheets and…The idea sent little tingles down her spine. 'You're not living with me.' She really hoped he couldn't hear that croak in her voice.

'All right, if you want to be accurate about it—that you have a flat in a house belonging to a single man.'

'Now who's fishing?'

'Me.' He spread his hands. 'So. I want to know. Are you single or attached?'

'That's irrelevant.' And she couldn't breathe when she saw the expression in his slate-blue eyes.

He felt it, too.

That weird pull of attraction.

This wasn't going to happen. She was six years older than he was, she was a country girl and he was definitely a city boy— and she wasn't in the market for any kind of relationship anyway.

'I could ask Grace,' he said thoughtfully.

'She wouldn't tell you.'

'Yes, she would,' he corrected.

'If you're insinuating that she'd tell you because you're paying her more than I could, then you're going to be disappointed.' Grace was her own woman; she couldn't be bought. And despite the fact Grace shared Jack's taste in music, her loyalties wouldn't switch that quickly.

'That's not what I meant,' he said softly. 'I think she'd tell me because she cares about you. If you're single she's probably worrying about you, and if you're attached, my guess is that she's already given your man the once-over. To see if he's good enough for you. And if she didn't approve she'd be stroppy with him.'

Alicia flushed. Jack had hit the nail right on the head. And she didn't want him talking to Grace about her love life. Because she knew Grace would be only too ready to interfere and suggest the same thing to Jack that she had to Alicia herself: a mad fling. 'I'm single,' she muttered.

Another quirk at the corner of his mouth. 'Good.'

Oh, dear. She needed to change the subject. And fast. 'When are your removal people coming?'

'They're not.'

She frowned. 'Why not?'

'Because I have a flat in London, and because I bought this place furnished.'

'So you're not going to live here?'

'Yes and no.' He glanced at his watch. 'Is there a good pub around here?'

'The Green Man, in the village.'

'Paddy's pub, I assume?'

She nodded, impressed that he'd remembered the name of Grace's boss from the conversation on Monday—and that he'd made the connection so fast.

'Right. Lock up—I'll drive.'

'What do you mean, you'll drive?'

'I'm taking you out to lunch,' he said.

'Why?'

'Because,' he said, 'I want to talk to you, it's nearly lunch-time and I don't have any food indoors. So either we have lunch out, or I'll be grumpy all afternoon due to lack of carbs. Oh, two more questions. Firstly, does Paddy's place have tables outside where we can eat?'

'Yes.'

'And does Saffy get car sick?'

'No.'

'Good. I'll put the roof of the car up while you lock the front door.' The question must have been written all over her face because he added, 'Saffy's coming with us. Your chaper-one, to make you feel a bit better about the idea of having lunch with me.'

She didn't even have time to ask him if he minded dog hair

being shed all over his car. Because he'd already handed one set of keys back to her and whistled to the Labrador—and Saffy was trotting happily behind him to the car.

Given that he'd already won her dog over, she had little choice but to fall in with his wishes. So she locked the front door of Allingford, grabbed her handbag from her flat and locked her own front door, and joined him in the car.

'Keys,' she said. The second time she'd given them to him.

'Thanks. You direct me,' he said. 'And you can choose the music.'

He had a state-of-the-art sound system. The first playlist was full of the kind of stuff Grace liked, loud and fast rock. And then there was another full of classical piano pieces. And then she discovered one with the kind of acoustic, ambient stuff she liked.

'Good choice,' he said when the music filtered through the speakers. 'Perfect for a chilled-out Saturday afternoon.'

She didn't feel particularly chilled out right at that moment. But she directed him to The Green Man and followed him into the garden, where he chose a quiet table in a corner under a parasol. She accepted his offer of a drink—grapefruit juice mixed with soda water over ice, because no way was she letting a drop of wine pass her lips and lower her inhibitions—and buried herself in the menu.

'Any recommendations?' he asked.

'It's all good.'

'Worried about being seen in public with me?'

That made her look up. 'No. It's not as if we're on a date.'

'No.' That quirk was back again. Along with a wicked glitter in his eyes. 'You'd know if it was a date.'

She knew it was a trap, but she still couldn't stop herself asking, 'How?'

'Because,' he said, his voice low enough for only her to

hear, 'you'd be sitting a lot closer to me. My arm would be round you. And I'd be whispering in your ear, telling you exactly what I was going to do to you when we got home.'

The vision that thrust into her head made her temperature rocket. To the point where she needed a gulp of her long, cold drink. And promptly choked on it.

He patted her back until she'd stopped coughing.

'That,' she told him primly, 'was completely uncalled for.'

'Sorry.' He didn't look in the slightest bit repentant. 'I was trying to make the point that this is just lunch. No strings.'

No-strings, hot sex. The phrase flashed into her brain and sent her temperature skyward again.

'And we'll go halves on the bill.'

'No. I asked you to lunch, so it's my bill,' he said. 'You can pay next time.'

There was going to be a next time?

'What do you fancy?'

Him.

And it was going to be much more difficult to put a lid on her feelings than she'd expected.

'Still looking,' she mumbled.

'Don't look at the prices when you choose,' he directed. 'Pick something you really want.'

She looked up just in time to see another teasing glint in his eyes.

He *knew*, damn it. He knew just what effect he had on her. The same as he would on any woman. Half the women in the pub's garden were staring at them, and it had nothing to do with concern about her coughing fit and everything to do with the fact that the man sitting opposite her simply *exuded* sex.

She was glad of the breathing space when he went to order their meals.

'I'm not sure I can cope with him, Saffy,' she told the dog—

who'd positioned herself exactly between their two chairs. Jack Goddard seemed to take charge of things without effort.

What she couldn't understand was why she was letting him do it. She'd always been independent—even more so, after Gavin. So why was she just going along with what Jack said?

She was very aware of the second he walked back into the garden, even though her back was to the pub. And that was another question: why was she so aware of him? Why had her senses gone onto a completely different pitch where Jack Goddard was concerned? She'd been engaged to Gavin, for pity's sake, and she'd never felt that tingle at the back of her neck whenever he was near. Whereas with Jack, the tingle started at the back of her neck and slid all the way down her spine before curling into her stomach.

Lust.

And she was old enough and wise enough to know better.

Alicia took another gulp of her drink—this time without choking on it—and Jack slid into the seat next to hers.

She needed to get control of the situation. Now. So she asked, 'What was it you wanted to talk to me about?'

'There isn't an easy way to ask this.'

Fear churned in her stomach. Please don't let him be about to ask her to move out. To give up her flat. She wasn't *ready*.

'It's going to sound incredibly tactless, so I apologise in advance.'

She frowned. 'What?'

He spread his hands. 'OK. You asked. I was wondering if you'd be able to keep an eye on Allingford for me when I'm not there.'

Her frown deepened. 'You're not moving here full time?'

He leaned back in his chair. 'I'll need to be in London some of the time, and there's a fair bit of work that needs doing to the house as well as the changes to the stable block. I want someone I can trust to keep an eye on the place. Someone who loves it. As I said, it's not tactful of me to ask, but you're the best person.'

'I…' He'd blindsided her again. This was the last thing she'd expected.

'You don't have to make an immediate decision. But that's not all I wanted to talk to you about.' He paused. 'When your flat's rewired you'll need to move out temporarily.'

Move out. Now those were the words she'd been expecting. 'Can't the electricians work round me?'

'No,' he said baldly. 'And rewiring means there'll be plaster dust and the need for redecorating afterwards.'

'I can live with that.'

As if he'd guessed her fears, he said softly, 'I didn't mean move out of Allingford. I meant stay in the main bit of the house while your flat is being sorted.'

He was inviting her to be his guest?

She couldn't quite get her head round this. 'You're going to get the wiring done.'

'And the damp problem. And the roof. And, yes, before you say it, I know there are rules for listed houses. Which is why I'm employing a builder who specialises in restoration work and knows exactly what he's doing. And I'm looking for an interior designer.'

An interior designer?

Everything was going to change.

She must have spoken out loud, because he said, 'Mmm, I thought orange and lime green would be a good colour scheme. Bit of leopardskin, and maybe zebra-striped carpet on the stairs…' Then he smiled. 'You should see your face. I'm *teasing*.'

She could tell that, now he'd stopped deadpanning. There was a distinct twinkle in his eyes. All the same, she wasn't amused. 'It's none of my business what you're planning to do with the house.'

'True, but I'm not going to force you to be overseer while I make huge changes. And I was joking about the colour schemes. I want something I can live with. Something restful. And you have to admit that the curtains and the soft furnishings need replacing.'

She shrugged. 'They've been like that since I was a child.'

He waited.

'OK. They've probably been like that since my dad was a child,' she admitted.

'Well, I'm sorry. I don't want to sprawl out on a lumpy sofa. I want something comfortable.'

She tried to blank the mental picture of him sprawled on a sofa with his head in her lap, listening to music while she read a book. 'Your interior decorations are none of my business.'

'I'm not looking for a London designer. If I'm going to be part of the community, I need to support local craftspeople. So do you know anyone locally who does interior design?'

Yes.

Someone who'd drawn sketches of Allingford as it could be, when she was a student. Someone who had the kind of vision she thought Jack would like.

And this would be a chance for Alicia to return a favour. Give Megan some of the support that Meg had given her over losing her father and her brother.

'My best friend's a partner in an interior design business. And she loves Allingford.' She paused. 'Except she's six and a half months pregnant, so this might not be the best time.'

'Would she talk to me, at least? Give me a quote?'

Megan would take one look at Jack Goddard and join forces with Grace. In fact, it wouldn't surprise her in the slightest if Meg and Grace had already discussed it. But she wasn't selfish enough to back out now and let personal stuff get in the way of her friend's business. A redesign at Allingford would be a dream commission for Meg and her business partner, Lorna. 'I'll ring her.'

'This afternoon?'

'This afternoon.'

'Good. When do I get to meet Bert? Will he still want to work in the garden?'

'I don't know to the first, and probably to the second.' She frowned. 'Do you always do everything at speed?'

'I don't dither and have regrets, if that's what you're asking. I make decisions and act on them.' All of a sudden there was a glitter in his eyes. 'Though I admit that some things are best done slowly.'

He didn't elaborate on it—but he didn't have to. She knew exactly what he meant.

Making love.

And suddenly she couldn't breathe.

Oh, God. She had to get sex off her brain. Jack Goddard was not, absolutely *not*, going to be her man to do.

She was relieved when the waitress brought their meals. And even more relieved that the waitress wasn't Grace; though she also knew that the girl was a friend of Grace's and would pass on the gossip immediately, which meant she'd have a few knowing texts later today. From Megan as well as Grace, because Grace would definitely tell her about it.

'Excellent food,' Jack pronounced.

'Up to your city boy standards, then?'

'Most of the time I don't actually have lunch. It's a sandwich at my desk, between meetings and conference calls.' He raised an eyebrow. 'Just as I'd bet that you forget to have lunch when you're working.'

'Well—yes,' she admitted. And she was relieved he'd

brought up the subject they hadn't talked about yet. 'Am I still able to work in the garden?'

'You told me you weren't the gardener,' he reminded her.

'I'm not. But—'

'—you love it,' he finished. 'And it's going to be hard for you to walk past a border and see a weed without taking it out.'

'Yes,' she said quietly. 'If I still have access to the grounds, that is.'

'Of course you do.' He looked surprised. 'Didn't you read your tenancy agreement?'

No. It had choked her too much. She'd just trusted her family solicitor to look after her interests.

'You can do what you like in the garden. Though I was thinking that maybe you should pay me.'

'Pay you?' She thought he was teasing. Or had she misheard him and he was trying to pay her?'

He leaned closer. 'I was thinking, in kind.'

Oh-h-h.

Every single nerve-end was tingling with the possibilities. 'I don't think that's legal.'

'What, making you give me a kiss for every weed you twitch out? No, but you're very teasable. Delectable. Delicious. De-lissy.' He leaned back in his chair, cut off a piece of grilled chicken and sneaked it under the table to Saffy. 'So am I allowed to call you "Lissy"?'

'Only my friends call me that. And you just fed my dog without asking.'

'Grilled chicken.' He wrinkled his nose. 'Sorry. Force of habit. I do the same with my parents' dog. My mother tells me off, too. I'll ask, in future.' He paused. 'So am I your friend?'

'I hardly know you.'

'That,' he said, 'is fixable. Very fixable.' He smiled.

'How?'

'We spend time together. Talk. Do things.'

It was the 'things' that worried her.

Just what did he have in mind?

He sighed again. 'Don't ever play poker, Lissy. Because you'll lose horribly. I can see the panic in your face. Look, we might as well stop pussyfooting round this. I'm attracted to you—and I think it's mutual.'

'What makes you think that?'

'Because your eyes go wide and your voice goes breathy when you talk to me. And you're wearing a T-shirt.'

One that didn't hide the fact that her nipples were erect. That she was turned on, fencing with him like this. She felt the colour shoot into her face and immediately crossed her arms across her breasts. 'A gentleman wouldn't mention things like that.'

'I'm not a gentleman. I'm *nouveau riche*. Though I've worked for my money.' He raised an eyebrow. 'I tell it like it is. And I'm right: it's mutual. I want you, Lissy, and you want me all the way back.'

'That doesn't mean we have to do anything about it.'

'Not immediately,' he agreed with a smile. 'But it's going to happen. When the time and the place is right. And it's going to be very, *very* good.'

CHAPTER FOUR

ALICIA wasn't quite sure how she got through the rest of lunch. Her body was on full, tingling alert. And it got even worse when Jack drove her back to Allingford; she was aware of how close he was to her, every time he changed gear and his left hand moved near her thigh. And when they got back to the house, it would be so, so easy for him to lean over and—

Oh-h-h.

She needed a cold shower.

Fast.

Jack didn't actually touch her. But he was thinking about it. She could see it in his eyes. Just as she could see that he knew she was thinking about touching him—that she was imagining what it would be like to slip her hands under the hem of his T-shirt and let her palms glide up his back, feeling his muscles move beneath her fingers.

'Thank you for lunch,' she said, striving to keep her voice as cool and calm as she could.

Your voice goes breathy when you talk to me.

She hated the fact that he was absolutely right.

'Thank you for agreeing to keep an eye on the house for me when I'm not here.'

It would've been more sensible to say no. Reducing the

contact between them. But how could she refuse to look out for the house she'd loved ever since she could remember?

He handed her one of the sets of keys. 'And you're going to ring your friend about the interior design stuff.'

'Megan.' She nodded. He was clearly about to ask her when, so she added, 'I'll do it now.'

He fished his mobile phone out of his pocket and handed it to her. 'Here, use this. You're calling for me so it's not fair to make the call on your bill.'

The phone was still warm with his body heat.

And she was practically hyperventilating when she rang Megan. It took a real effort to speak normally. 'Meg? It's Lissy.'

'Are you OK? Do you need rescuing?' Megan asked immediately.

'What?' Did she sound that panicky? Did pregnancy suddenly make you a mind-reader?

'This isn't your mobile phone number,' Megan explained.

'No, it's…' Alicia took a deep breath. 'I need to introduce someone to you. Someone who wants to talk to you about a possible design commission.'

'A big one,' Jack whispered, his breath fanning her ear.

He was doing this *deliberately*. Although he was referring to the commission, she was well aware of the innuendo. The fact he'd whispered in her ear made it even worse. She glowered at him, wrapped one arm around her breasts because she just *knew* he was going to stare at her nipples, and moved away slightly.

'Meg, I know the timing isn't brilliant because you'll be on maternity leave soon, but…' She swallowed. 'His name's Jack Goddard.'

'You mean Jack Sex-God?'

'You *know* him?'

'No-o.'

Megan sounded as if she was squirming, and Alicia knew exactly who'd given him that nickname. The same person who'd no doubt told Megan all about her brilliant idea for Alicia to have a fling with him.

She'd murder Grace later.

'He'd like to talk to you about redesigning Allingford.'

'Are you sure about this?' Megan asked doubtfully. 'I mean, yes, I'd love to do it—of *course* I would, it'd be a dream job for anyone—but I won't do it if it's going to make you feel awkward or rub your nose in the fact it's not yours any more.'

'Meg, those drawings you did when we were students…you love this place. I think you and Lorna would be the right designers for it.' And Jack had enough money to make their visions come true.

'Are you sure about this?' Megan repeated.

'Absolutely.' Because whatever she said to Jack Goddard, the redesign was going to happen—and Alicia would rather that Allingford was in the hands of someone who loved the house than be left to the mercy of some designer who'd see it as just bricks and mortar. 'I'll hand you over to him.' She turned to face Jack. 'You'll be talking to Megan Hart. It's best that you speak to her yourself, as you know when you're free for a meeting and what have you. And I have things that need doing so I'll get out of your way. Thanks for lunch.'

Aware that she was being a complete coward, she forced herself to walk slowly to the corner.

And then she raced Saffy for her front door.

When she heard Jack's car on the gravel, some time later, she waited five minutes, and then headed out for the garden. She spent the afternoon attacking weeds and digging out some of the border, but all the while his words were echoing in her mind. *It's going to happen. When the time and the place is right. And it's going to be very, very good.*

And every time she thought about it, her heart gave a funny little flip.

There was no sign of him for the rest of the afternoon. She was aware that he'd returned in the early evening, because Saffy sat to attention by the front door, but to her relief there was no knock. He'd taken the hint and was going to leave her in peace.

She was working on some exam practice questions for her students after a meal of a toasted cheese sandwich when there was a knock on her door.

When she opened the door, Jack was leaning against the door-frame. Looking utterly gorgeous. 'Howdy, neighbour,' he drawled.

'Hello, Jack.' Oh, that was good. She sounded cool and calm and in control. Exactly how she didn't feel.

'I want you to come for a walk with me.'

She frowned. 'What?'

He looked through the open door at the table where her laptop was open and there were files stacked next to it. 'Are you incredibly, screamingly busy, or can you spare me about a quarter of an hour? You and Saffy, that is?'

She should say no. Really she should.

Except Saffy had heard the W-word and was already standing underneath the hook where her lead hung, wagging her tail madly. If a dog could smile like a human, then Saffy was beaming from ear to ear around her beloved teddy bear.

'Sure.' Alicia clipped the lead onto the dog's collar, then locked the front door behind her.

'Thanks for putting me in touch with Meg. She's very nice.'

'Yes. She is. And she's happily married with a three-year-old and a baby due in a couple of months.'

He laughed softly. 'You don't have to warn me off her. I never mess about with married women. She's coming to see me on Monday and we'll have a chat about how she thinks it could work.'

'She's really good at her job—and I'm not just saying it because she's my best friend. She did some sketches of Allingford when we were students, and they were amazing. It made me see the house in a whole new light.'

'Hmm,' Jack said thoughtfully.

It was a perfect evening, with the full moon rising above the lake; the stars were out and not a single cloud obscured their view. The light was so bright that it was practically as good as daylight, and Alicia could even see the expression in Jack's eyes.

An expression of wonder.

'This is incredible,' Jack said softly. 'The moon reflected in the lake, and the stars—you never see this in London. And that bright star over there…'

'…is actually a planet,' she corrected. 'It's Venus.'

Then she wished she'd kept her mouth shut. Venus. The goddess of love. Jack would think she was trying to come on to him.

'So you know about astronomy, too?'

'A bit. If you can see it twinkling, it's a star—otherwise it's a planet. We've had the most amazing views of comets before now. Hale-Bopp was like a thumbprint smudged across the sky. And the lunar eclipse last year was stunning—you really could see the moon turn red and the "diamond ring" flashing as the last bit of the earth's shadow went across the moon.'

He smiled at her. 'Your parents were interested in stars as well as plants, then?'

Parents? She gripped Saffy's lead more tightly. 'My father was the one who brought me up.'

He grimaced. 'Sorry, I didn't realise your mum was dead.'

'She isn't. I lost the wrong parent.' The words were out before she could stop them.

Jack took her hand and squeezed it. Gently. Like a hug. 'Want to talk about it?'

'No. Let's just say we're not on brilliant terms.'

'Then I'm sorry for hurting you, dragging up things you'd rather not remember. That really wasn't my intention.' Another gentle squeeze, and he let her hand go. 'I just wanted to share this view with someone because it's so beautiful.' He dipped down and patted the grass. 'Oh, damn. It's damp.'

That made her smile. 'You're such a city boy.'

'I'm not bothered about me. I was thinking about *you*. I'm sure you'd rather not get your jeans damp.' He sat down and looked at her. 'I don't have a blanket—but you *could* sit on my lap.'

At her silence, he chuckled softly. 'Coward.'

'I thought you just wanted me to see the view?'

'I do. It's when you're near me…' To her surprise, he sang the few bars of 'The Nearness of You'. And his voice was gorgeous—low and soft and sexy.

And the words he was singing…

It made her knees weak. She had to swallow hard. 'You're a born charmer,' she said, striving to keep her voice light.

'Hardly. My dad loves Hoagy Carmichael and George Shearing and Nat King Cole, and I was brought up on their records.'

'And you play them on the piano as well?'

'Well, yes,' he admitted. 'My dad's a piano teacher.'

'So that's how come you play so well.'

'Thank you.' He acknowledged the compliment with a smile. 'And that's also how come I know I don't actually want to be a musician—I love music and I like messing around on the piano, but I really don't want to spend hours and hours practising. And I don't want to have to play the same piece in the same way every single time. I play for fun. It relaxes me.'

She made the mistake of looking into his eyes. Which told her exactly what else relaxed him.

'Don't look so worried,' he said softly. 'I'm not going to leap on you.'

She wasn't sure whether that made her feel more disappointed or relieved.

'I was telling you about my family. Dad's a music teacher and Mum's a PA—she keeps everyone organised.' He spread his hands. 'There's a rumour that I inherited her bossy gene.'

'Never,' Alicia deadpanned.

He laughed. 'Only when I have to be. And, being the youngest, I'm used to being bossed around at home.'

She scoffed. 'I can't imagine anyone bossing you about.'

'I didn't say they succeeded,' he said with a grin. 'They just try. My brother's the oldest. Lee. He's a computer technician and a complete nerd.'

Alicia glanced at him. From the look on his face, Jack was obviously close to his brother, the same way she'd been to Ted. Respected him. Probably teased him stupid about mathematical concepts, but also went out for a beer and to concerts with him, enjoying his company.

'My sister's the middle one. Cathy. She's a nurse. Oh, and she's married to my best friend.'

'The music journalist?'

He looked pleased that she'd remembered. 'Yes. Cathy's only a year older than me, and so is Jimmy—he took a gap year before university. Our first Christmas holidays, he came to stay at our place for a few days, met Cathy and fell for her like a ton of bricks.' He pulled a face. 'It's kind of weird, having your best friend date your sister. But he fits right into our family. And I suppose it made my best man's speech a bit easier at the wedding.'

The way Jack talked about his family, with such love and happiness in his face...Alicia really envied him. She'd lost the two people she loved, and she was left with the woman who'd never wanted her in the first place.

Well, that went both ways. She didn't particularly want Rosalind, either.

Some of her thoughts must have shown on her face because suddenly Jack stood up again and slid his arm round her shoulders, hugging her. 'Hey, I wasn't trying to say I've got everything you haven't and lording it over you.'

'I know.' But being this close to him was playing havoc with her synapses. She pulled away.

'What's wrong?'

'I'm not looking for a relationship, Jack.'

'Neither am I. So where's the problem?'

'I…' How did she explain it?

'Look, there's something there between us. I can't stop thinking about you. And it's the same for you.'

Yes. Not that she was going to admit that out loud.

'So the sensible option,' Jack said, 'is to get it out of our systems. Hot sex. Lots of it. No strings.'

Almost exactly Grace's words. She really, really hoped Grace hadn't emailed Jack to thank him for the CD and then suggested it.

'Until one of us has had enough,' he said softly.

And that was the problem. According to Gavin, she wasn't much good at sex. And Jack would have had enough of her long before she'd grown tired of him.

She'd already lost too much. And she wasn't willing to take any risks, lose more. 'No.'

'Talk to me,' he said softly. 'Tell me what the problem is.'

'Nothing.'

'I know from my mum and my sister, when a woman says "nothing" it means "nothing I want to tell you" or "nothing I think you'll want to listen to". So tell me,' he coaxed. 'Tell me and we'll work it out between us.'

She swallowed. 'I know I said I don't want a relationship—

and I don't. But I also don't want to see someone who's got a ton of other women.' She lifted her chin and stared straight at him. 'I've been there, done that, and I have no intention of repeating my mistakes.'

His eyes glittered. 'While I'm with you, I won't see another woman. I'm not good at sharing, either—so the same would go for you.'

Something in his voice alerted her. 'Been there, done that?' she asked.

'Yeah. Add in flashy wedding and ver-r-ry messy divorce. Not to mention expensive.' His voice was wry. 'Thing is, if you want a rich husband, you have to expect him to work long hours to earn said money. Especially in the early stages of his career.'

So clearly his ex-wife had been fed up with waiting around for him to come home from work, and had found herself someone who'd give her more attention—while at the same time enjoying the lifestyle that Jack worked so hard to give her. 'That's rough.'

He shrugged. 'You can kiss me better, if you like.'

'We're not having a relationship,' she reminded him.

Another shrug. 'OK. So it's your turn to tell me about him. The guy who cheated on you.'

Gavin. It had been eighteen months, now. She'd stopped missing him, stopped loving him. But the hurt was still there. And the anger at herself for being such a fool, for trusting him and not seeing what was going on under her nose. She did her best to keep her voice expressionless. 'He was a lecturer at the same college. My fiancé. Except he was seeing one of his students.'

Jack's eyes narrowed. 'So he abused both your trust and his position. The worst kind of coward. You're much better off without him.'

'I know.' But she'd lost confidence in her judgement of men, and she really didn't want to get hurt again.

'So. We've both been hurt.'

'Yes.'

'But we both feel this weird kind of pull towards each other.'

'I didn't say that.'

'You didn't have to,' he said softly. 'It's in your eyes. They're saying exactly what I'm feeling. I never normally mix business and pleasure, but I can't stop thinking about you. So what are we going to do about this?'

She swallowed hard. 'You said, hot sex until one of us has had enough.'

'Uh-huh. When it's out of our system. And then we let the other one down gently. Really, *really* gently.'

'This feels like negotiating the terms of a relationship.'

'Not exactly. More like setting some ground rules. We've both been hurt and we both want to avoid it in the future. So working out some ground rules would be sensible.'

'Hmm.' She still wasn't sure where this was leading.

'I don't want to get tied down again, and neither do you. I'm attracted to you, and you're attracted to me. We both want the same things. So I think we might be good for each other.'

'Do you always talk people into doing what you want?' she asked.

'A lot of the time, yes.' A faint smile curved his lips. 'But I don't have a lot of talking in mind right now.'

'I don't think I can do this.'

'Not ready? Fine. I'll wait.'

Now, that she hadn't expected. 'You don't strike me as a patient man.'

He laughed. 'I'm not. But I'm also not stupid. I know when something's worth waiting for.' He rubbed the pad of his thumb over her lower lip, and her mouth tingled. 'So I'll wait.' His gaze held hers in the moonlight. 'Just not too long.'

CHAPTER FIVE

JACK stood looking out of his bedroom window. He didn't think he'd ever get bored with the view. Right now, in late spring, the bluebells were out in a carpet under the trees, all different shades of blue and purple and white dappling the ground. There were ducks and geese on the lake. And the rhododendrons were just starting to come out.

He could understand exactly why Alicia loved this place so much. He'd fallen for it himself, the moment he'd seen the details. And the house had more than lived up to his expectations.

He glanced down at the formal garden. As he'd half-expected, Alicia was there, on her hands and knees, with gloves on to protect her skin from thorns and stings, twitching weeds out of the border. She'd clearly been working for some time, as the wheelbarrow next to her was full. And although it was only April, it was really warm. She must be sweltering.

On impulse, he went down to the kitchen, poured a mixture of orange juice and sparkling water into a jug, added ice, then put the jug and two glasses on a tray and took it out into the garden.

'Good morning,' he said. 'You look hot.'

He'd meant as in temperature.

But as soon as the word was out of his mouth he realised she might take it the other way. Which was also true—even in old jeans and a T-shirt with her hair pulled back in a scrunchie, she made his temperature go up a few degrees—but last night he'd promised to give her space. To be patient. Right now she was vulnerable and he shouldn't push her—even though he still wanted to kiss her.

'As in it's a good twenty degrees out here and you're working in full sun,' he added swiftly. 'I thought you might like a drink.'

'Thank you.' She took off her gloves and accepted the glass from him; for a second, her fingers touched his and all his nerve-ends fizzed.

God, he really had to keep himself under control.

And watching the movement of her throat as she drank was not a good idea. It sent too many flickers of lust through him.

To calm himself down, he took a long swig from his own glass, then sat on the lawn and made a fuss of Saffy. 'So this is maintenance, yes?'

She nodded. 'If you do it every day, you get the weeds before they grow too big and start spreading seedlings. Leave it, and you've got a monster to deal with. Though I have to admit, weeding isn't exactly my favourite activity.'

He couldn't resist the question. 'So what is?'

She blushed, very slightly.

Good. That meant she was thinking the same thing that he was. Favourite activity: kissing. Touching. Tasting. Making love…

Heel, boy, he reminded his libido.

'Planting,' she said. 'Except I suppose I need to talk to you about that.'

He put his glass on the tray and held both hands up in the traditional 'surrender' gesture. 'Hey. You do what you think fit.'

'Seriously?'

'Seriously. I know nothing about gardening—apart from having to water the tomatoes in my dad's greenhouse when I was a kid, to earn my pocket money.' He spread his hands.

'Whereas you're an expert. So just tell me what's needed and I'll set up an account at whatever plant centre you suggest.'

'Thank you.'

For a moment, he thought she was actually going to cry. There were definite tears in her eyes. Much as he wanted to give her a hug and tell her everything would be OK because he was here, he resisted the temptation. If he held her close, he couldn't promise himself that he'd be able to stop himself taking it further.

'I'll catch you later, then,' he said. 'I'll leave the drink here for you.'

And he left before he did something rash. Like hauling her into his arms and kissing her stupid.

So Jack was going to let her have her garden after all?

She could've thrown her arms round him and kissed him.

But she knew it wouldn't have stopped at kissing. And it was complicated: from what he'd told her, the previous evening, his ex-wife had taken him to the cleaners, even though she'd been the one to break up the marriage with an affair. It was hardly surprising, then, that he didn't want a relationship. With something like that in his past, of course he'd have trust issues. And if Alicia had kissed him straight after he'd told her she could have her garden and he'd set up an account at the nursery of her choice… Well. It would have felt as if she were only doing it as a kind of payment.

Which wouldn't have been the case at all. She wasn't like that.

Though it was all academic, because nothing was going to happen between them anyway.

She shoved the thoughts to the back of her mind and concentrated on the weeding. And it wasn't until her stomach rumbled and she glanced at her watch that she realised it was three o'clock.

Definitely late for lunch.

Just as well she only had herself and Saffy to please.

She dumped the garden refuse on the compost heap, put the wheelbarrow back in the orangery, and had just reached her front door when she saw Jack. He was alternately studying a piece of paper and glancing around. She frowned. What was he up to?

Before she could say anything, Saffy bounced up to him and swiped him with the teddy bear.

'Hey, beautiful.' He didn't push the dog away or make a fuss about yet another muddy smear—though admittedly his jeans looked old and faded anyway. He made a fuss of the Labrador, then glanced over to Alicia. 'Hi. Finished for the day?'

'Stopping for lunch.' Now he'd given her the go-ahead to restore the garden, she thought she'd done more than enough weeding to reward herself with some work on the garden plan.

'It's a bit late for lunch.'

She shrugged. 'I'm fine. What are you doing?'

'Planning where the stage should go.'

She frowned. 'Stage?'

'For the concert.'

'But I thought…' Her voice trailed off.

He smiled at her. 'It's not going to interfere with your garden. I want the lake as the backdrop to the stage and the fire-works. And probably a marquee of some sort in the lawn.'

'The lawn by where I've just been working?'

'Yes. That's the obvious place.' He looked surprised for a moment. 'If you're worrying about people accidentally walking on the garden, don't. I'll have temporary fencing put up—bright orange polyethylene mesh that people won't be able to miss, held up with steel fencing pins that we can take out afterwards. It's reusable so all we have to do is add some reflec-tive barrier tape on the top and round the pins.'

'A marquee.' She still couldn't get her head round this. 'With people trampling round.'

'On the *lawn*,' he emphasised. 'And lawns are for walking on, are they not?'

She ignored his smile. 'It's not a lawn. It's the site of the garden.'

He frowned. 'I'm not with you.'

'You said this morning I could do what I liked with the garden. I was going to restore the original gardens. So that isn't actually a lawn.'

'It's an area covered in green grass. That makes it a lawn, in my book.'

'It's the site of an important garden.'

He rolled his eyes. 'A garden that doesn't exist.'

'A garden that *did* exist. We've got historical evidence.' Exasperation made her sharp. 'Just because you bought Allingford, it doesn't mean you own it!'

He folded his arms, with the map or whatever it was held between his arm and his chest. 'Funny, that. I thought the law of property meant that I did.'

She shook her head in frustration. 'You're splitting hairs. Yes, you bought the property and the land. But that doesn't give you the right to rip everything up. You're the custodian of the house for the next generation.'

'Interesting.' His voice was very, very cool. 'Considering that the last custodian was allowing the place to slide very genteelly into ruin.'

He might as well have driven a fist straight into her stomach. All the air left her lungs, and she was reduced to glaring at him until she could catch her breath. 'That's below the belt.'

'It's also true,' he pointed out. 'So don't tell me what to do with *my* house.'

There was nothing she could say to that.

And if she stayed here she'd say something she really regretted. Better to walk away, now. So she whistled her dog to heel—much to her disgust, Saffy's head drooped as she returned to Alicia's side—and went into her flat. And she banged the door very, very hard behind her.

Alicia was too angry and upset to eat lunch. And it was clear to her that it would be pointless working on the garden plans now. So much for thinking that she and Jack had an understanding. And how the hell she could be attracted to such a two-faced, lying creep…

She'd been dead right about millionaire businessmen being ruthless and single-minded.

That was Jack Goddard, all over. Rich, ruthless and resolute on doing something that would ruin the house. Sure, she could do what she liked—as long as it didn't interfere with his plans. He'd been patronising her all the way along.

And right now, she didn't want to kiss him. She wanted to throttle him. For being an insensitive, overbearing, pigheaded…

Arrrgh.

A cool shower didn't improve her mood.

And neither did cleaning her flat; she didn't manage to scrub the tension away.

'Which leaves us two choices,' she informed Saffy. 'One, we go to the beach.' A run would probably help get rid of her anger—though she didn't trust Jack not to have changed his mind now about letting her go where she liked in the grounds. The last thing she wanted was for him to accuse her of trespassing, so the beach was safer. Firstly because it was miles away, and secondly because the calm, rhythmic swoosh of the waves would soothe her. 'Or two, I bake.' Comfort food. Cookies and cakes. The scent of vanilla and chocolate always made her feel brighter, and she didn't have to eat the lot herself; she could take some into the staff room at college tomorrow and it would no doubt disappear before lunchtime.

Saffy just remained curled up in her basket with her nose

on her paws. Clearly the row had upset her; she wasn't used to disharmony. Even when she'd found out the truth about Gavin, Alicia hadn't yelled her head off; she'd simply walked quietly away.

Whereas right now she was absolutely seething.

'Cooking it is, then.'

So she mixed and stirred and kneaded and took out her temper on the dough she was making. And as her anger cooled from molten lava to more of a simmer she started to think that maybe she'd been out of line. Jack had said some pretty cruel things to her—but she'd started the fight. She'd been the one to throw a hissy fit.

Bottom line: Allingford was his, now. He could've refused to let her stay in the flat or touch the garden at all; the fact that he'd let her stay and continue her work was a lot more than many other people would have done. He'd behaved decently, and she'd thrown it all back in his face.

Maybe, she thought as she took a tray of cookies out of the oven, she'd take some of these over to him later. Apologise. Try to smooth things over between them.

Just as she was thinking that the doorbell rang.

Odd. She wasn't expecting anyone. Unless Megan had decided to come over and find out what she could about Jack before their appointment to talk about the interior design work. Though right now Alicia probably couldn't say anything nice about him.

She opened the door and stared in surprise. Jack was leaning against the doorjamb. 'We need to talk.'

'What about?'

He sighed. 'You know what about. May I come in?'

Despite her good intentions of making up with him, she still resented the fact he'd dangled the garden in front of her and then snatched it away again. 'You're the landlord. I can hardly refuse you.'

'I thought we were becoming friends, Lissy,' he said softly.

'We were.' Or had been, until their fight.

Clearly she was still furious with him. The high colour in her cheeks wasn't just because of the heat of the oven—from the gorgeous scents emanating from her kitchen, he was pretty sure she'd been cooking something. 'I apologise for what I said. It wasn't fair, because I know you love the house—you just didn't have the money to sort everything out.'

'Most of my salary went on the house, actually.'

And that bothered him. The house hadn't been left to her, when her father died. It had been left to her brother. Ted had been the one who should've been responsible for the house. So why had he left his sister to deal with it?

He asked her straight. 'What about Ted?'

She shrugged. 'Expeditions to the rainforest don't come cheap.'

No, and Ted hadn't paid much of the inheritance tax bill either, according to Jack's solicitor. Which made him think that the only reason any of it had been paid at all was because Alicia had organised the sale of the paintings and other valuable items. 'So the responsibility's been landed on you for years.' So although what he'd said was true—Allingford was falling into ruin—it wasn't her fault. She'd done her best. Tried her hardest. And taken on her brother's obligations. 'That makes what I said even more unforgivable.'

'I was just as rude to you. I apologise, too. I said things I shouldn't have done.'

'We were both angry.' And he knew exactly why. 'Frustration,' he said softly.

'I beg your pardon?'

He didn't repeat it; she'd probably have another hissy fit on him and deny it. Instead he smiled and said, 'Truce?' He took his hands from behind his back and handed her a bunch of flowers.

She looked at them and then at him. 'Are these from the borders?'

He spread his hands. 'There aren't any shops open at this time of day on a Sunday. Are you going to yell at me for picking them?'

'From your own garden?' She smiled wryly. 'Hardly. They're lovely. And I normally cut some tulips so I can enjoy them indoors as well as in the garden. Thank you.' She paused for a moment, as if deciding what to do. 'Do you want to come in for a cup of coffee or something?'

Or something.

No, that wasn't on offer. And if he kissed her now she'd *really* slap his face. He'd much rather she kissed him back. Which meant continuing to be patient. 'Thank you.' He closed the door behind him and sniffed appreciatively as he followed her into the kitchen. 'Have you been baking?'

She gestured to the cookies cooling on the rack. 'Help yourself.'

He did, and bit into one. She was definitely as good a cook as she was a gardener. And she was neat, too; the kitchen was compact, with a bistro table and two chairs, but there was no clutter anywhere. No doubt her living room and bathroom were the same.

He wasn't going to let himself think about her bedroom.

Or how much he wanted her, naked, against smooth cotton sheets.

By the time she'd finished arranging the flowers, the kettle had boiled and the coffee had brewed. She didn't ask him if he took milk or sugar; clearly she remembered his tastes from the last time she'd made him coffee.

A woman who paid attention to detail.

And the way Allingford was sliding into disrepair must have driven her crazy.

Time for an olive branch. 'The cookies are very good.'

'Thank you.'

She was clearly still wary of him. And from their row he knew that the root of it was the garden. But why was it so special to her? There was only one way to find out. 'Talk to me about the garden.'

Her eyes narrowed. 'What's the point?'

'Because I get the impression you're usually cool and calm, and we had a slanging match earlier.'

She flushed. 'I've already apologised.'

'So have I. Don't stress about it.' He waved a dismissive hand. 'Why is the garden so important to you?'

'Because it's something I've always wanted to do—restore it to how it was when my family first came here.'

'You said you have documentary evidence.'

'Yes.' She grimaced. 'Actually, it really belongs to the house.'

'Was it in the inventory?'

'No.'

Therefore she hadn't really needed to tell him anything about it. Which meant she was honest, too.

He really should stop judging women by Erica's standards.

'If it's not in the inventory then it's not legally mine,' he said.

'But it's documentary evidence about the house.' She frowned. 'It belongs with the house really.'

But clearly she hadn't been able to part with it. 'May I see it?'

She nodded and left the room, returning with a leather-bound book. 'Would you mind putting your coffee on there, please?' She gestured to the worktop, then checked that the table was dry before taking a piece of paper from the book and unfolding it.

As soon as he looked at it he realised it was a map of Allingford. The hall was at the centre, and the gardens were drawn in detail. 'This is the kind of thing you don't touch without gloves on, right?' he asked.

'Right.' She flashed him an approving smile. 'The journal was made by Alicia Beresford—the first one to live in the house. I was named after her.'

That didn't surprise him. 'She was a gardener, too?'

Alicia nodded. 'It's in my blood. Dad and his rhododendrons, Ted and his rainforests…and me and the garden here. This journal contains all the planting plans and Alicia's description of the garden during the seasons as it grew. She illustrated it with watercolours.' She handed him the journal.

He glanced through it, careful to touch the edges of the page and not the print. 'Wow. This is beautiful. Have you thought about getting this published? You know, a facsimile sort of thing?'

'That was part of the plan. *After* I'd restored the garden.' She raised an eyebrow and nodded at the map. 'You can see the layout properly here. Here's the lake, the formal garden, the orangery, the walled garden…and here's the Italianate garden.'

Exactly where the lawn was.

And he hadn't seen a trace of it. Just a wide, flat lawn. 'So how come it disappeared completely?'

'It seemed that a great-great-whatever was apparently keen on croquet. And because the area was the perfect size and it was flat, he wiped out the garden for his croquet lawn.' She grimaced. 'When I came across the journal in the library, with the map, I could hardly believe it. I've made a copy of the map so I have a working copy I can make notes on, but I thought you should see the original.'

Because it clearly meant the world to her and she wanted him to feel the same enthusiasm about it.

'You know you asked me if I thought about opening the garden to the public?' she queried. 'Once I'd restored the old garden, I planned to open it. And I want to run a module at the college on garden archaeology, starting in the next academic year—I was intending to use Allingford as a case study.'

Which she would've done, had she still owned the place. But when Ted died, not only had she lost her last remaining close family, she'd lost her dreams as well. Because the garden was no longer hers to restore.

He could let her do it. And he could feel all noble and self-sacrificing and smug about what a kind person he was.

But then he'd lose his own dreams. And he didn't want to give them up.

There had to be some sort of compromise. 'Could you still do the module without restoring the garden?' he asked.

She shrugged. 'I suppose. Though it's not going to be the same.'

Her world was so different from the one he'd come from. And he wanted to know more. Wanted to know what made her tick. 'So what do you actually teach?'

'The core subjects for the HND and degree in horticulture—basic principles and practice, pests and diseases, and plant nutrition, growth and development,' she explained.

Hmm. Her dad had bred rhododendrons and her brother was a botanist. She'd loved them both. So although she'd said gardening was in her blood, he couldn't help wondering. 'Did you want to be a gardener for *you*? Not just to please your family and fit in?'

'I wanted to do it for me.'

He could tell from her face that she was being sincere. She probably had fabulous memories from her childhood, all involving gardens. And even though he knew he was on dangerous ground, he couldn't stop himself asking, 'Was your mother a horticulturalist, too?' Was that how she'd met Alicia's father?

Distaste flickered briefly on Alicia's face. 'She didn't like plants any more than she liked planets. God only knows why she married Dad. Because of the house, I suppose.'

He knew how that felt. Erica had pretty much done that, too. Persuaded him to move to an expensive London town house, dangled the prospect of a family…and all the time she'd been seeing someone else. He'd given her the house as a divorce settlement and walked away.

'Rosalind was a city girl through and through. She loathed it here—later, Dad told me she always said it was a backwater. It was OK before she was pregnant with Ted, when she could do the country-set stuff and go to balls and have dinner parties. But Dad—I mean, you almost *never* saw him in a suit.' Alicia shook her head. 'He was happiest in these baggy, scruffy cords and a checked shirt and wellies, working in the greenhouse. He wasn't into dinner jackets and cummerbunds. They were just too opposite for it to work.'

Was this an oblique way of telling him she didn't think it would work between them, either? That he was a city boy and she was a country girl and they'd never find any common ground?

'I was barely even a year old when Rosalind left for London.'

'Rosalind' again, he noticed, rather than 'Mum'. Clearly there wasn't much love lost between them. That was something he really couldn't understand; he and his siblings were close to their mother, and knew she loved them all dearly.

'She didn't take you with her when she went?'

Alicia shrugged. 'Babies weren't a good fashion accessory at the time—and I would've curtailed her social life too much. So she left me with Dad and Ted. But I don't have any issues about it, before you ask. I would've hated it in London, being passed from nanny to nanny or stuck in boarding school. Whereas I grew up here knowing that I was loved.'

And that, he thought, accounted for her inner strength. The certainty that her father and her brother had loved her—the same kind of love he'd had in his own family. And he was glad she'd had that. 'Do you still see her?'

'Not unless I really have to. Funerals and weddings, basi-cally.' Alicia's face shuttered. 'When I was eighteen, she wanted me to go and live with her and come out into London society.'

Which would've gone down like a lead balloon, he knew. 'And you said no?'

'Yes, but Dad said I ought to go. He said I should mend bridges, give it a try for a while before I went to university—because she was my mother. Even though she'd never acted like a mother to me.' She smiled grimly. 'I lasted all of three days.'

'It was that bad?'

She nodded. 'Party after party after party. And all the time people spoke *at* each other, not to each other. They talked about nothing. And they were always looking round to see if there was someone more important to talk to.'

Ouch. That was probably true of most of the parties he'd been to, too.

'It wasn't for me. So I pleaded a headache when Rosalind wanted to go on this shopping spree. I wrote her a note while she was out and got the train back to Norwich, then rang Grace's grandmother and talked her into coming to pick me up. Grace was a toddler at the time—she was delighted because it meant she got to come with her grandmother and see the trains. She made choo-choo noises all the way home.'

He laughed. 'I can imagine that.' And that explained perhaps why Grace had seemed so protective of Alicia. Because she was clearly almost like family.

'But before we got back, Rosalind had found my note and blistered Dad's ear. He didn't make me go back again, but she was furious with me for wrecking all her plans to buy me designer clothes and show me off like a trophy. She was even less pleased when she found out I was going to do a degree in environmental biology. She thought I should do something like media studies.' Alicia sighed. 'But Dad stuck up for me and said it was important to do what you love and love what you do. That's worth more than all the money in the world. Do what makes you *happy*.' She paused. 'Is that why you're taking a sabbatical from hedge-fund management?'

'I'm not planning to swap it for hedgerow management, if that's what you're asking. I liked my job.' It wasn't quite his passion, but he was good at it and he enjoyed it. Just, right now, it wasn't enough of a challenge for him. He was looking for something more. 'But I've got to the stage where I want to do something for me. Chase a dream or two. Do something a bit different.'

'The country house recording studio.'

He nodded. 'And the concerts.'

'With a marquee smack in the middle of the g—'

He reached over and pressed his forefinger to her lips. 'We're not going to have another fight today.'

Her mouth parted slightly, and his pulse sped up. Was she going to draw his fingertip into her mouth? He could feel the warmth of her breath against his skin. See the flicker of desire in her eyes.

Yes.

And then she took a step backwards, breaking the connection. 'All right. No fighting.' She gave him a wry smile. 'I was going to come and see you, actually. Apologise. Bring you cookies as an olive branch.'

'Beat you to it.' With flowers she'd grown herself. Not quite the same. 'I don't want to fight with you, Lissy.'

'I don't want to fight, either.'

'Then let's just let things settle for a while. See how things go.' He held out his hand; she took it, and shook it.

Except he wasn't quite ready to let go. Instead, he lifted her hand to his mouth. Pressed his lips lightly against the pulse in her wrist. Kept his gaze very firmly fixed on hers, so she could see exactly what he was feeling. 'Later,' he said softly. It was a promise.

Then he left—while he still had enough self-control to do so.

CHAPTER SIX

MEGAN, like Grace, took a real shine to Jack. 'He's a nice guy,' she told Alicia, the day after her meeting with Jack. 'And he's drop-dead gorgeous.'

'And what does that have to do with anything?' Alicia asked.

Megan just laughed.

'I really don't know why you and Grace are trying to fix me up with him. I'm perfectly okay as I am,' Alicia protested. 'I don't need a relationship to be happy.'

'Lissy, you're *not* happy,' Megan said gently. 'And it's not just because of the house. I think you need someone to share your life.'

'I already have. I've got Saffy.'

'I meant human company,' Megan said. 'You're lonely.'

'Just because you're happily married with one-and-a-bit children, it doesn't mean that everyone else wants to be like that,' Alicia grumbled.

'I know that, but Jack's lovely. And I think he'd be really good for you.'

Alicia rolled her eyes. 'You sound just like Grace. I bet she's shared that ridiculous idea of hers with you.'

Megan laughed again. 'Actually, it's not so ridiculous. She has a point.'

'You do know what his plans are for this place, don't you?' Alicia asked.

'Yes. And I think it'll be good for the house, actually. It needs people.'

Just what Alicia had thought herself. Except she hadn't been thinking about lots of people, she'd been thinking of a family.

A family she didn't have and wasn't going to have.

Just for a second, Alicia envied Megan. She had it all—a job she loved and a family she loved. Simon adored her; he was a brilliant father to their little girl, he'd be a brilliant father to the new baby, and he would never let Megan down the way that Gavin had let Alicia down.

She pushed the thought away. She wasn't lonely, and she didn't need a husband and children to feel fulfilled. She was doing just fine on her own. Except…'I'm not going to be able to restore the garden,' she said, biting her lip. 'Jack has other plans for the area.'

'I'll tell him I can't take the commission,' Megan declared immediately.

Alicia shook her head. 'Meg, don't do that. I'm not that selfish.'

'If it's going to make things hard for you, I won't do it. You've been my friend too long for me to let work get in the way.'

'I know. But you'd love to do the redesign, wouldn't you?'

'It's a dream job,' Megan admitted.

'So do it.' Alicia smiled at her. 'It's why I recommended you to him in the first place. Not only will you do a brilliant job, you'll really enjoy it. So do I get a sneak preview of your plans?'

Megan winced. 'I hate to say this, but…'

'Client confidentiality. I know. I shouldn't have asked,' Alicia said swiftly.

'I'm sorry.' Megan looked awkward and embarrassed.

'No, it's my fault. I shouldn't have put you on the spot. Forget I said anything.' Alicia switched the conversation back to babies, luring Megan off the scent, and enjoyed the rest of her evening with her best friend. But after Megan had gone, Alicia curled up on the sofa with Saffy and thought about it.

Was she lonely?

She didn't miss Gavin any more—once she'd realised he was a lying cheat who only cared about himself, her love for him had vanished. But if she let herself think about it, she had to admit she missed the companionship. She missed sharing her life with someone other than her beloved dog. She missed being held, being touched.

Jack Goddard had offered it to her on a plate. *Hot sex. Lots of it. No strings. Until one of us has had enough.*

'I must be deranged,' she informed Saffy, 'to even *consider* it. A fling with Jack Goddard would be completely the wrong thing, for a hundred different reasons.' And yet the more she thought about it, about his gorgeous blue eyes and sensual mouth and hard, fit body, the more she was tempted.

'Definitely deranged,' she said.

On Wednesday afternoon, Jack heard the soft roar of a motor and frowned. It sounded like a lawnmower. Bert was way too old to be mowing the lawns, especially lawns the size of Allingford's; even though the mower he'd seen in the orangery was a ride-on one, there was still all the business of hauling bags of grass-cuttings about. He'd go and have a word with the old man and see if he knew anyone who might be able to take the job on for him—a young lad who wanted to earn a bit of extra cash, maybe. Or perhaps one of Alicia's students would do it.

To his surprise, when he rounded the corner he realised that Bert wasn't the one using the ride-on lawnmower. It was Alicia.

But it was too early for her to be home from college. Shouldn't she be at work?

She was driving the machine in his direction. He started to

walk towards her, lifting one hand in a bid to snag her attention; she waved back and when she was within a metre of him she switched the lawnmower to idle and stopped.

'What are you doing here?' he asked.

She gestured to the swath of cut lawn behind her. 'What I do every Wednesday afternoon.'

'But aren't you supposed to be lecturing?'

'Not on Wednesday afternoons. That's earmarked for student sports—football, rugby, cricket and so on.' She gestured towards the wide lawns. 'And it means I get a chance to keep this lot all under control. If you leave it more than a week, especially if we've had heavy rain, it turns into a complete jungle.'

'That looks like fun,' he said, eyeing the lawnmower.

Worry crossed her face. 'It's not like quad biking, you know.' Then her eyes widened. 'Please tell me you're not thinking about doing that on m—*the* lawns,' she corrected herself swiftly.

He was tempted to tease her and tell her it was a fabulous idea...but he really didn't want another fight with her. Especially as she'd caught herself before she said 'my lawns', showing that maybe she was beginning to accept the situation. Instead, he said, 'Don't you think I should be doing this?'

'Why?'

'Because,' he said softly, 'it's my responsibility now.' She'd already had to do too much on her own in the past.

'You just want to play with the tractor, don't you?'

'Tractor?' It didn't look like one to him. 'It's a ride-on lawnmower, isn't it?'

'This baby is a garden tractor, I'll have you know,' she corrected.

'So what's the difference?'

'It does mulching as well as cutting.'

'Which means?'

'The short answer is that it recycles the grass cuttings so you don't have to get rid of them. Which, in the case of Allingford, is about nine tons a year,' she explained.

That was a *lot* of grass. 'I've got a lot to learn about this,' he said wryly. 'And given what you do for a living, you're exactly the right person to teach me. Talking of which, I really ought to pay you for the work you're doing in the garden.'

She shook her head. 'It's not a job.'

No. For her, it was a labour of love. His heart ached for her. Letting go of Allingford really wasn't going to be easy for her. Not when she'd been in control here for so long.

'Why don't you let me help you? You can start by giving me a lesson on how to use this thing.'

'Boys and their toys,' she said, rolling her eyes, but she got off the tractor, indicated to him to sit on the seat, and talked him through the controls. She was all very efficient and effective, but a far more irresistible idea slid into his mind. The seat was adjustable, which meant it would slide back. And that meant there would be just enough room...He adjusted the seat, leaned over, caught Alicia round the waist and hauled her onto his lap.

'What are you...?' she began, sounding shocked.

'My first time, I can't possibly steer *and* do the gears *and* do the pedals,' he said, telling her a blatant fib, 'so I thought maybe you could steer and keep me in a straight line while I get used to the rest of it.'

'This is against all health and safety regulations,' she warned, but he was pleased that she hadn't pulled away.

It wasn't going to be *that* dangerous. He had no intention of driving particularly fast or trying to do any kind of stunt driving. He could tell that driving the garden tractor actually *wouldn't* be that much different from driving a quad bike—which he'd done a few times before—so he didn't really need any instructions from her: but this was too good an opportunity to pass up. Having her sitting on his lap, up close and personal. Near enough for her to feel the heat of his body—and to start getting used to the idea of him being this close to her. So he just smiled and wrapped his arms round her waist, pulling her back against him.

She smelled gorgeous—of roses and lavender—and she was warm and soft and touchable. And she was steering the tractor, so all he had to do was to keep his foot on the accelerator…and let his mouth stray to within millimetres of the curve of her neck.

Although she was talking him through what he was supposed to be doing, Jack wasn't paying much attention to what she was saying. He was more intent on the quality of her voice, how it was becoming higher and breathier as she spoke. She definitely wasn't immune to him, any more than he was immune to her. He deliberately fanned his fingers against her midriff, and her voice went breathier still.

Good.

But it still wasn't enough. Although her T-shirt was thin cotton, it was still a barrier. He wanted to touch her. Skin to skin. Now. He couldn't wait any longer. So he hooked his little fingers under the hem of her T-shirt and slowly drew the material upwards.

Oh-h-h. At last. The touch he'd craved. Warm, soft skin. It felt fantastic. But he wanted more.

Much more.

He took his foot off the accelerator, bringing the tractor to a halt, and brushed his mouth against the curve between her neck and her shoulder. Alicia shivered and tipped her head back against his shoulder. Unable to resist, Jack moved his hands higher, cupping her breasts underneath her T-shirt. Her bra was lacy, the material rough against his fingertips, and he could feel her nipples hardening through the lace. He rubbed the pads of his thumbs over them, and she took a sharp intake of breath. Again, good: she was enjoying this as much as he was.

'Lissy.' His own voice was a good octave lower than usual.

'We shouldn't be doing this. There are people about. Bert's working in the walled garden.'

Her self-control amazed him. She was incredible—all the physical signs told him that she was really turned on, and yet her head was still clear enough to take in the situation and be aware of what was going on around them.

He wanted that self-control to splinter into the tiniest fragments.

And he wanted to be the one who splintered it.

He wanted to be the one who made Alicia Beresford see stars bursting.

'There's nobody to see us,' he said softly. 'The walled garden is the other side of the house, and the builders won't be back until next week. It's just you and me.'

'This really isn't a good idea,' she croaked.

'Why not?' He nibbled her earlobe, and she gave a tiny—and very gratifying—murmur of lust.

'I'm six years older than you.'

'So?' He wasn't bothered by the age difference between them. What was six years? 'You're thirty-four. Hardly in crone territory.'

'And—' she dragged in a breath '—you're my landlord.'

'So?' That didn't bother him either. It should do, he knew, but it didn't.

'It makes things complicated.'

'Actually, it's very simple.' He drew her even closer against him. 'I want you.' He was pretty sure she knew that; as she was sitting on his lap, she must be able to feel his erection pressing against her. 'And it feels as if you want me too.' Apart from the fact that her nipples had peaked, the beat of her heart was so strong, so fast, he could actually feel it pounding against his fingers.

Her breath shuddered. 'I…'

'You're right,' he said. 'This tractor thing wasn't a good

idea. Because I don't have quite enough room to turn you round to face me. And I want to kiss you, Lissy. I really, really want to kiss you. Properly. Hot and wet and hungry.' Just to show her, he glided his mouth from the hollow behind her ear, all the way down to the collar of her T-shirt. She shivered and tipped her head back, offering her throat to him.

'I've been thinking,' he whispered, 'about you and me. About lying out here with you, under the stars. Just you and me and a blanket, making love in the moonlight. You'd look like some kind of moon goddess, your skin like alabaster as I uncovered every inch of it, stroked you, touched you, *tasted* you.'

She wriggled on his lap, rubbing against him and making him catch his breath. 'Jack. You're driving me crazy.' Her voice was husky with desire.

'You drive me crazy, too. So why don't we do something about it?'

'I…' She was suddenly hesitant.

'Scared? I'm not going to hurt you, Lissy.' This was the first time he'd seen her with her hair loose, and he loved it; it was naturally straight, not flattened with irons. He nuzzled the strands aside to bare the nape of her neck and kissed her skin lightly. 'Let's find out how good it can be between us,' he said softly.

She shivered. 'Not here.'

'Where?' He knew he was pushing her. But he really needed to know.

'I…' She shook her head in apparent frustration. 'I'm never this inarticulate.'

'Then doesn't that tell you something?'

She leaned her head back against his shoulder and bit her lip. 'I'm not very good at this sort of thing.'

The whispered admission sliced at his heart. 'Says who?'

'It doesn't matter.'

He could guess. The guy who'd been cheating on her. It

didn't take a huge leap of imagination to realise that he'd probably used it as an excuse to justify his behaviour—and Jack was furious on her behalf. So furious that it was a real effort for him not to clench his fists. He wanted to break the cheating, lying bastard's jaw. 'Ever considered that he might have been wrong?' There was no 'might have been', in Jack's eyes: it was a definite. Alicia wasn't in the slightest bit frigid. She'd been so responsive to his touch. 'They say that attack is the best form of defence, so he was probably trying to cover up the fact that *he* wasn't any good at it.' And Alicia was clearly inexperienced enough to have believed the man's lies.

'Maybe.'

She'd tensed up. He continued to hold her close, hoping that maybe the warmth of his body would relax her. But when her back remained rigid, he sighed and brushed a kiss against her shoulder. 'I'll prove it to you. And we'll both enjoy it. But you're right—here and now isn't the right place.' Gently, he restored order to her clothes, then slid his arms round her waist again. 'Come on. Let's finish this lawnmowing business.'

Driving the garden tractor with her on his lap was surprisingly enjoyable. It worried him slightly that he enjoyed her closeness as much as he'd enjoyed touching her. This was meant to be a physical thing, getting it out of their systems so they could just carry on with life as normal. He wasn't going to get emotionally involved.

Neither of them were.

Alicia made him stop the tractor before they returned to the walled garden, and slid off his lap.

'Worried about Bert?' he asked, raising an eyebrow.

'He's known me for years.'

'And?' He didn't follow.

'I don't want any…speculation.'

In other words, she didn't want to be teased. 'Fair enough. This is just between you and me.'

'Just between you and me,' she echoed.

'And, just so you know…' he held her gaze '…it's only going to get better.'

CHAPTER SEVEN

ALICIA spent a very hot and bothered night, full of X-rated dreams. Dreams of Jack touching her, kissing her, easing his body into hers. Now she knew his touch, it made the visions in her head even more vivid.

Even a cool shower the next morning couldn't get the images out of her brain. She was distracted all day at work, and by the time she got home she was beginning to think Jack was right about this. The only way to deal with the crazy attraction between them was to get it out of their system. Have a blazing affair. Let the whole thing burn itself out. And then life could go back to normal.

Plus there was something weighing on her mind. The journal. She'd photographed every page, and the camera, computer and printer she'd bought were good enough to let her reproduce the originals with sharp clarity. Much as she hated to give up the journal, she knew that morally it belonged to the house more than it belonged to her.

So she might as well kill two birds with one stone.

She'd give Jack Alicia's journal.

And she'd say yes to the mad fling.

Later that evening, after she'd taken Saffy for a walk round the lake, she settled the dog in her basket. 'Sorry, honey. You can't come with me this time,' she said, rubbing the top of the Labrador's head. 'I'll make it up to you later. Promise.'

Then she took a deep breath, tucked the journal under her arm and rang Jack's doorbell. It felt weird, ringing the bell of a door she was so used to opening herself with a key, but she wasn't going to take liberties with the set of keys he'd given her. They were strictly for use when he was absent, and only if it was necessary.

He'd obviously just had a shower, because his hair was still wet when he answered the door. And it was all she could do not to leap on him there and then.

'Hi. What can I do for you?' he asked.

Kiss me. Take me to bed.

She swallowed hard. 'Just being neighbourly.'

He smiled. 'Actually, I was coming to see you anyway.'

Her heart missed a beat. To finish what they'd started yesterday afternoon?

'It's going to start getting a bit noisy round here from next week.'

'How do you mean?' She didn't understand.

'The builders are going to be in. It'll be a while before work can start on converting the stable block, because I'm still waiting for the permission to go through, but we can start on the work that needs to be done in the main house because we're not actually altering anything—we're doing essential maintenance, and the planning people know that I'm using one of the builders on their list of restoration specialists.'

'Isn't there a waiting list or something?'

'I was lucky. There was a cancellation—so they were able to fit me in,' he told her. 'The electrician is going to start work on rewiring your flat on Monday. Which means that you need to move out temporarily.'

'Where to?'

He rolled his eyes. 'I thought we'd already sorted that, Lissy. You're moving in to my bit of the house while the work is being done on your flat.'

'I could stay in Ted's flat,' she suggested.

'No, because it makes sense to have that done at the same time as yours. Otherwise it'll be really noisy for you, while his place is being renovated.'

She could hardly argue with that.

'Are you working at the college, this weekend?' he asked.

She shook her head. 'I work every weekday except Wednesday afternoons. I tend to mark assignments and prepare lectures and tutorials at home.'

'Good. I'll give you a hand on Saturday to move your stuff. Which room would you like?'

This was her cue to say 'yours'.

Except when it came down to it, she chickened out.

'Whatever you think best,' she said, as coolly as she could manage.

A beat of silence passed. A beat in which she couldn't help thinking about sharing a room, that bed, with him. A thought that she knew he shared, because his gorgeous blue eyes widened slightly. Just for a second, she could see desire blazing from his gaze.

'I'm in the room overlooking the lake,' he told her.

The master bedroom.

So he was giving her the choice.

Share a room with him, or insist on her independence.

'I'll take the one at the end of the corridor by the back stairs,' she said immediately.

The corner of his mouth shifted slightly. She knew full well that he was mentally calling her a coward, because she'd chosen the room that was the furthest possible from his.

And then he was back to being the affable host. 'Do you need me to get you any boxes? And before you say it, yes, I know you're quite capable of sorting it out for yourself. But you're at work during office hours, and my time is a bit more flexible.'

It was a fair point. One she was happy to concede. 'But why Saturday?' she asked. 'Why not Sunday?'

'Saturday morning to pack, Saturday afternoon to move your stuff and get you settled in, and Sunday to see if there's anything else you need before the electricians start work on Monday.'

Sunday to spend all day in bed with him. The idea sent a shiver of desire all the way down her spine.

'Then thank you. I could do with some boxes,' she admitted. 'How much do I have to move?'

'Everything. We can move your furniture into the dining room, temporarily.'

She nodded. 'How long do they think it will take?'

He shrugged. 'As long as it takes. It depends what they find while they're doing the rewiring—if anything else needs to be fixed. And then we need the plasterers in afterwards to redo the walls, and the decorators to spruce everything up again.'

'So I could be staying with you for weeks.'

'Is that a problem for you?'

'No, but won't it…well…cramp your style?'

He raised an eyebrow. 'Why would it do that?'

She felt colour slide into her face. This was a bad, bad move. And although she'd thought that a fling would help, now she was having second thoughts. Serious second thoughts. If she did have a blazing affair with him, it might only last a few days. She and Grace had already agreed that Jack Goddard would be good at sex. He looked the sort. And he was probably used to having really, *really* good sex. When he found out she wasn't…then it would be over. Fast. Which would leave her feeling really awkward, and a definite gooseberry when he found someone else. And he might feel awkward, too, at bringing someone else home while she was staying there. 'I…' She bit her lip. How did she explain this without looking like an idiot?

He took pity on her. 'I'm single. You're single. It isn't a problem. Unless you'd rather I found you alternative accommodation?'

'No.' Please let her find the right words to tell him.

He laughed wryly. 'Why are we having this conversation on the doorstep? Come in. And I think it's my turn to make you a coffee. Where's Saffy?'

'Dozing in her basket.'

He ushered Alicia inside and then shepherded her through to the kitchen. Which looked rather different from the last time she'd been in the room. For a start, there was a very expensive-looking sound system on one of the worktops. And then there was an enormous American-style fridge in place of the little fridge and freezer that she'd left there.

Clearly he saw the surprise on her face because he smiled. 'I hate to say it, but your fridge was really on the way out. I would've offered it free to a good home on one of the recycling websites, but I don't think it'd meet regulations.'

Just like most of the electrical equipment in Allingford. She didn't dispute it.

'And it didn't have an ice maker.'

She couldn't help smiling back at him, remembering his enthusiasm when he'd seen the garden tractor. 'You just like gadgets, don't you? Boys and their toys.'

'Not just the gadgets. It's useful to have the storage space.'

She scoffed. 'There's only you. Why do you need a huge fridge?'

'I don't, at the moment,' he said affably. 'But I will do.'

She remembered his plans for the recording studio and people staying at the house. 'Sorry, it's none of my business.'

And it wasn't why she was here, anyway. 'I brought you this.' She held out the journal.

He didn't move to take it. 'Why? It was your great-great-great-whatever grandmother's.'

'But it's part of the house's history.'

'It's also part of your family history. You're her direct descendant. It belongs to you.' Forestalling her protest, he took her hands and folded them round the book. The pressure against her hands was light, but the contact made a shiver of desire run all the way down her spine. Made her wonder what it would be like to have his hands against other parts of her body—stroking down her spine, the curve of her buttocks. Made her remember what it was like to have his hands touching her midriff, gliding up over her breasts, teasing her nipples.

How could blue eyes look so *hot*? she wondered. Because right at that moment Jack's did. And his mouth had parted.

He was going to kiss her.

The kiss they would've shared this afternoon on the garden tractor, if she hadn't been such a wuss.

'Jack,' she whispered.

Without a word, he took the book from her and placed it on the table. Then he cupped her face with both hands; his fingers were strong and firm and warm against her skin. His thumb rubbed against her lower lip, the way it had the night they'd sat beside the lake in the moonlight. Her lips parted, and she drew his thumb inside her mouth, sucking gently.

His breath hissed sharply from him. 'Are you sure you know what you're doing, Lissy?'

No. But she was going to do it anyway. In answer, she tipped her face up slightly, inviting him to kiss her.

And he did.

He dipped his head so that his mouth touched hers. Teasing and inciting. Tiny nips of his teeth, nowhere near hard enough to hurt but firm enough to tell her how much he wanted her. The tip of his tongue soothing where his teeth had been, showing her that he would be gentle with her.

She slid her arms round his neck, pulling him closer. Opened her mouth beneath his. And murmured into his mouth in pleasure when his tongue slid between her lips, tasting and exploring. Just the way she wanted his body to slide into hers.

Oh, Lord.

She'd never wanted anyone this much before. So much that she felt she was going to spontaneously combust. She could feel herself growing wet between her legs; as if Jack instinctively knew it, he wedged one thigh between hers. But it still wasn't enough. She needed more.

Just as he'd done on the garden tractor, he slid his hands under her T-shirt. But this time he stroked her back rather than her midriff. He moved his fingers in tiny circles all the way up her spine, until she was quivering and so desperate for him to touch her properly that she nearly pulled back and ripped her own T-shirt off.

And then she felt him unhook her bra.

One-handed.

Panic filled her. Obviously he was a man who'd done this before. A lot. He knew what he was doing—and he would quickly make exactly the same discovery as Gavin had done. That she just wasn't good enough at this sort of thing. She'd never match up to his previous lovers.

As if he sensed her sudden doubts, he pulled back far enough to look straight into her eyes. 'What's wrong, Lissy?'

'You're a lot more experienced than I am.'

'And that's a problem, how?' His tone was kind.

'I'm going to disappoint you.' The admission almost choked her.

Gently, he took her chin between his thumb and forefinger

and tipped it up until she met his eyes. 'You're not going to disappoint me. In fact,' he said, 'I'm going to enjoy this. A lot. Because I plan to introduce you to all sorts of things your sleazebag ex obviously didn't bother to do.'

She felt a hot tide of colour wash into her face. 'Why are you so sure that it was all his fault?'

In response, he took her hand and placed it on his chest. 'Can you feel that?' he asked.

The strong, steady beat of his heart.

She nodded.

'The way you just kissed me back did this to me.' Still keeping his fingers twined with hers, he drew her hand slowly down his abdomen. Lower still. Down and down, until her hand was curved around the distinct bulge of his erection. Proving beyond all doubt that he was aroused.

The heat in her face increased even more.

'It did this to me as well,' he said softly. 'You turn me on in a big way, Alicia Beresford. And I'm going to enjoy doing exactly the same for you. Turning you on until you can't think straight.'

He had already. Her knees were beginning to feel distinctly wobbly.

'I'm going to enjoy stroking you all over,' he continued. 'Exploring you, finding out where and how you like to be touched. How and where you like to be kissed. And I'm really going to enjoy seeing exactly what you look like when your self-control splinters into little tiny pieces and you come so hard you don't even know which universe you're in.'

There was a pulse beating hard between her legs and she had the nasty feeling that she was quivering. And that he knew it. If he so much as crooked his little finger, she'd follow him upstairs to his bed and spend the entire night making love with him.

He dipped his head again and brushed his mouth against hers. 'But waiting,' he whispered, 'makes it even better.

Because you're going to be on a slow burn from this moment until we finally go to bed. You're going to be so *hot* for me…' his eyes glittered '…so hot, that the only way you're going to be able to cool down is by ripping your clothes off and wrapping your body around mine.'

'Hot sex. Lots of it.' She remembered exactly what he'd suggested when they'd had lunch at the pub. A suggestion she hadn't been able to get out of her head.

His mouth curved. 'That,' he said huskily, 'sounds perfect.' He stole another kiss and stepped backwards. 'That coffee I promised you probably isn't a good idea.' His eyes were still glittering. 'Because I think my self-control is going to have a nasty habit of disappearing when you're around.'

She turned him on that much? The unexpected feeling of power was heady; she stopped thinking and just acted on impulse. 'So if I did this…?' She tugged at the hem of her T-shirt and pulled it off in one swift movement, removing her undone bra at the same time.

Colour slashed across his cheekbones. 'Hell, Lissy! I'm not a saint. I'm a man.'

Uh-huh. She knew that. And the bulge in his jeans told her that he was an extremely aroused man.

His tongue moistened his lower lip. 'Oh, God. You're gorgeous. You look like an angel. And I need to touch you, Lissy. Taste you.' He cupped her breasts, just as he had on the tractor. Except this time he could see as well as feel what he was doing. The pads of his thumbs rubbed against the hardened tips of her breasts, and the friction made her gasp.

'Do you like that?' he asked, holding her gaze.

'Yes,' she whispered.

'Tell me.'

'I like it.'

'Like what?'

She dragged in a breath. 'I like you…touching me.'

'So do I. You're beautiful, Lissy. Perfect curves. All woman. And right now, I really have to…Oh-h-h.' He bent his head and drew one nipple into his mouth. Alicia quivered. He teased the sensitive peak with the tip of his tongue, and warmth spread between her thighs. When he began to suck, her hands fisted in his hair.

'Jack. This is…' She searched for words and couldn't find them.

He lifted his head for a second. 'You like that?'

'Yes.' The word came out as a hiss of pure pleasure.

'Good.' His pupils had expanded so much that his eyes looked almost black. 'And this is only the beginning, Lissy.'

To her shock, he straightened up, retrieved her T-shirt and handed it back to her.

So did this mean he'd changed his mind?

Either she'd asked the question aloud or it showed in her face, because he shook his head. 'I haven't changed my mind. At all. But I want you to wait. I want you to be on a slow burn, so the moment my mouth touches your sweet spot, you're going to come. And I'm not going to stop until you've come again. And again.' Once more, he moistened his lower lip with his tongue, and she watched him, mesmerised, thinking about what he said and imagining how it would feel when the tip of his tongue glided along her clitoris.

She almost came just at the thought.

'Is that a promise?' she asked huskily.

'Yes.' He smiled. 'And something you should know about me. I always keep my promises.'

She pulled her T-shirt back on and tucked her bra into the pocket of her jeans. 'I hope so.'

'I'm a man of integrity,' Jack said. 'People know they can trust my word. It's why I do well in business. What you see is what you get.'

Unlike Gavin, who'd been one thing on the surface and quite another underneath.

'Me, too,' she said.

'I'm in London tomorrow. But Saturday,' he said softly, 'is going to be…' he took a step forward and stole another kiss '…good,' he whispered. 'Really good. For both of us.'

CHAPTER EIGHT

ALICIA spent the rest of Thursday night and the whole of Friday on a slow burn. Although she knew Jack was in London and she wasn't even sure if he was coming back that evening, she couldn't stop thinking about him. About the way he'd kissed her. The way he'd touched her. The words he'd whispered to send her pulse rate rocketing.

She just about managed to keep her concentration at work, but it was a close-run thing, and several of her students actually asked her if she was all right. Not to mention the lunchtime conversation with Megan, in which her best friend declared she was clearly on another planet.

She came home to find several large removal firm boxes stacked outside her front door; clearly Jack had had them delivered, so he'd made good on one of his promises. Her temperature went up several notches at the thought of how he'd make good on the other promises he'd made.

I'm not going to stop until you've come again. And again.

She tried to keep her mind off it by packing her books and papers and household effects, then labelling every box with its contents so she knew which ones she could leave until moving back into her flat and which ones she would need to unpack.

I plan to introduce you to all sorts of things.

Her imagination went into overdrive.

You're going to be so hot *for me.*

She was. And by Saturday morning, Alicia was a wreck.

Because today was the day.

The day when she moved back into the main house—and the day when she and Jack would make love for the first time. The day when they'd strip all the barriers away. The day when they'd explore each other, learn what made each other's eyes go wide with pleasure.

A cold shower just about got her libido under control. She toyed with her usual yoghurt and fruit at breakfast; she was too keyed up to eat properly, though at the same time she knew that she'd need energy for moving her stuff.

Not to mention energy for making love all night with Jack Goddard.

At nine o'clock, her doorbell rang.

Jack stood on the doorstep, looking sexy as hell. Like a fallen angel. He was wearing a black T-shirt with the logo of a band she didn't know, faded jeans that looked so soft she itched to reach out and touch them, and he clearly hadn't bothered shaving that morning.

And his smile was pure sin.

Saffy launched herself at him—the way that Alicia was tempted to do, but held herself back—and Jack made a fuss of the dog before turning to Alicia and saying, 'Good morning.'

'Good morning.' Her voice was croaky, and she hated the fact it gave her feelings away. Especially when he gave her a slow, sensual look that told her he knew exactly what had been going on in her head for the last couple of days—and it was precisely how he'd intended it to be.

She only hoped it had been the same for him.

'Thank you for the boxes.'

'No problem. The removal company said they'd drop them

off.' He smiled at her. 'I thought I'd turn up early and help you start packing.'

'Thanks, but I've already packed everything. I only need to finish taping up one box.' The one that contained her crockery; she'd just washed up her breakfast things, dried them and wrapped them in newspaper, and slotted them into place in the box.

'Then let's start moving them. Which ones are the heavy ones?' He gave her a sidelong look. 'And this is one of the few cases where I *don't* believe in equality. I'm bigger than you and I can carry heavier things than you, so you do just the light stuff and leave the rest of it to me, OK? No heroics.' He paused. 'Unless, of course, you really want to pull a muscle and to have me massage it for you.'

She really wished he hadn't said that. The idea of him giving her a massage, stroking her skin, made her nipples harden and set a pulse throbbing between her legs. And she could see from his face that he knew it.

'What about the furniture?' she asked. He couldn't manage that all on his own, surely?

'I have reinforcements coming to help me with that.'

His expression told her that he wasn't going to explain that remark, so she didn't bother asking. Though she didn't think he meant Grace; apart from anything else, she knew that Grace was working at the pub all day. And Megan definitely wasn't in any condition to be moving boxes or furniture. 'Which room are we moving everything into?' she asked instead.

'I thought the dining room. We can eat in the kitchen for the time being.'

We.

She really had to remember that this was only temporary. That this wasn't a relationship. That as soon as the electricians and the builders had finished, she'd be moving straight back into her own flat. 'OK,' she said.

'Do you want to start by taking your suitcase up to your room?' he asked.

Her room. The one she'd chosen—at the furthest end of the corridor from his. Would she be sleeping there tonight? Or would she be sleeping in Jack's bed?

He was clearly thinking the same thing, because there was a flash of heat in his eyes. She had to look away before she did something embarrassing. Like walking over to him, sliding her arms round his neck and jamming her mouth over his.

'Where's Saffy going to sleep?' she asked.

'Where would you prefer her to be?' he asked.

'She's used to being in the kitchen.'

'That's where my parents' dog always sleeps at home.' He ruffled the dog's fur. 'You'll be absolutely fine here, won't you, sweetheart?'

Saffy's tail thumped.

'It's going to be nice, living with a dog again,' he remarked.

'So you don't have a dog in London?'

'It wouldn't be fair. I live in a flat and I work stupid hours.' He shrugged. 'Some choices are harder than others. I still get a share in the family dog. Though it's not quite the same as having one around full time.'

They'd just about finished moving the boxes and cases when Alicia heard the sound of a car pulling up on the gravel. Saffy bounded out to the front of the house, carrying her teddy bear as usual, ears pricked; Alicia and Jack followed.

'Hey, there!' Jack greeted the driver of the car with a hug and hearty slaps to his back, and the other man responded in kind. 'How was the journey?'

'Let's just say I'm glad I had satnav and not Cathy directing me,' the visitor replied with a grin.

'Alicia, this is Jimmy. Jimmy, Alicia,' Jack introduced them.

She held out her hand to him. 'You're Jack's best friend and his brother-in-law, aren't you?'

Jimmy shook her hand, looking pleased that she knew who he was. 'Yes. And you're…' He stopped flushed. 'Sorry. I think I was about to put my foot in it.'

'I'm the house's previous owner,' Alicia confirmed. 'And no offence taken.'

'It's a fabulous building,' he said. 'I can see why Jack fell for it.'

'You wait until you see the grounds,' Jack said enthusiastically.

Alicia remembered that Jimmy was a music journalist. And no doubt he thought that Jack's plan to hold a music festival in the grounds of a country house was a good one. She still didn't, but right at this moment she didn't have the energy to fight.

'Why don't you go and unpack while we move the furniture, Lissy?' Jack suggested.

'Isn't there something I can do to help?' After all, it was her stuff. She really wasn't comfortable with the idea of leaving everything to Jack and Jimmy.

'I'm not sure if I dare ask.'

She felt her eyes narrow. 'What?'

'I'm not being sexist,' he warned, 'but a cup of coffee and a sandwich would really hit the spot right now.'

He thought she was going to pull him up for being sexist, just because he'd asked her to make them some lunch? She smiled. 'I think I can just about manage to lift a kettle and fill it.'

'I wouldn't challenge you to an arm-wrestle.' There was a mischievous twinkle in his eye, which told her he was thinking of a very different type of wrestling. And Jimmy had clearly picked up on the undercurrent too, because he was looking at both of them with undisguised interest.

'I'll call you when lunch is ready. Anything you want in particular?'

He waved a dismissive hand. 'Whatever's in the fridge.'

'Jimmy?'

'Same for me,' he said.

She headed for the kitchen. Saffy curled up in her basket and thumped her tail when Alicia glanced over at her.

'Yeah, it's good to be back,' Alicia admitted softly.

Jack's fridge turned out to have very eclectic contents. Skimmed milk, a drawer full of vegetables, a couple of bottles of freshly squeezed orange juice, a bottle of Chablis, a punnet each of strawberries and raspberries…and a drawer full of chocolate. She made a mental note: the man might have a clean-living lifestyle, but he was a hedonist at heart.

She couldn't resist a quick peek into the freezer. One whole shelf was taken up with premium ice cream. Several different flavours. A vision flashed into her head of both of them reclining back against the pillows in Jack's bed, sharing one of the tubs of ice cream and a spoon, and the pulse between her legs started to beat harder. Would they do that tonight? Make love, and then he'd pad downstairs to the kitchen, and raid the freezer…

She shook herself, looked through the cupboards until she found where he stored his bread, made a plateful of ham salad sandwiches, and then called Jack and Jimmy down to the kitchen.

Jimmy chatted to her about music and films and history; he was good company, easy to be with, and she took an instant liking to him. If Grace were here, she thought, they'd probably talk music until stupid o'clock and try to top each other with the most obscure bands they'd seen. But then again, if Grace were here, she'd no doubt pick up on the little glances between Alicia and Jack. Alicia only hoped that Jimmy, being male, wouldn't be quite as perceptive. And wouldn't ask the obvious

They stayed for just long enough to drink a mug of coffee and demolish the sandwiches between them.

'Right, back to work,' Jack said.

'Anything I can help you move?' she asked.

Jack shook his head. 'We'll handle it. You might as well unpack your stuff. Do you want to use the library as your office, seeing as it already has a desk?'

She blinked in surprise. 'My office?'

'Office. You know, a place for preparing assignments and marking—lecturer sort of things,' he said.

'Thank you.' She was touched by his thoughtfulness. 'But don't you need it?'

'It's big enough to share. We'll take your computer stuff in there, then.'

By the time she'd unpacked, they'd nearly finished moving everything and Jimmy was re-siting the desk by the window in the library. 'Jack said you'd prefer having a view,' he explained when Alicia walked in.

She nodded. 'The garden is important to me.'

'So he said.' Jimmy paused. 'You know, I haven't seen him this happy in years.'

'Since he was with his ex-wife?'

He raised an eyebrow. 'Jack told you about Erica?' He looked thoughtful. 'She pretty much broke his heart. Which is why none of his relationships last more than half a dozen dates nowadays.'

'Is that a warning?' she asked softly.

'Don't get me wrong. He's a good man. I'd trust him with my life. But he's so *restless*. Lives his life at a hundred miles a minute. He used to work stupid hours—and although he claims this is a sabbatical and he's loafing around for a few months, I don't believe a word of it. Look at the way he's launched himself into building plans and rewiring, and I bet he spends half his day on the phone, wheeling and dealing. He's keeping himself busy because there's something missing in his life.' Jimmy shook his head, looking sorrowful. 'He really needs the right woman to settle down with.'

'No, I don't,' Jack corrected, walking in with Alicia's flat screen monitor and clearing having overheard the last bit. 'I've done my time settling down, and I don't intend to do it again. Life is for *fun*.'

That, Alicia thought, was definitely a warning. Jack's way of reminding her that this was only going to be temporary. Yes, they were going to have a hot affair, but there wouldn't be any future in it. This was just gratification, and just for now.

And she'd better not let her heart get involved.

'Do you want to stay for dinner?' Jack asked Jimmy.

'Thanks, mate, but I need to get back to London.'

'What, so you can give your wife a full report on the house?'

'And your mum. They're bribing me with cake.' Jimmy laughed. 'You know, if you'd given us a bit more notice, Cathy would have come down to help as well.'

Jack grinned back. 'Why do you think you got such short notice?'

'You're going to have to give in and let them inspect it soon,' Jimmy warned.

Jack spread his hands. 'I sent them a huge pile of pictures by e-mail. What more do they want?'

'To see it in person and be nosy. You know what women are l—' Jimmy glanced at Alicia. 'Whoops. Me and my mouth. Present company excepted, of course.'

She laughed. 'I know quite a few women who fit that description, actually.' Starting with Grace and Megan. She knew she was going to get the third degree from both of them at some point during the next few days.

'Well, it was nice to meet you, Alicia.' He held out his hand to her.

'You, too.' She shook his hand warmly.

'I'll see you out,' Jack said.

When they'd left the room, Alicia started plugging wires into the back of her computer box and connecting it up to the monitor and peripherals. She was on her hands and knees under the desk, her backside in the air, when she suddenly felt a hand smoothing over the curve of her bottom. She jumped in surprise, her head came up and smacked against the desk, and she gave a startled yelp.

She ducked down again, rubbing her head, and crawled backwards from under the desk.

'Sorry, Lissy. Temptation got a bit in the way of my common sense. Are you all right?' Jack asked

'I'll live.' Some devil made her add, 'You can always kiss it better.'

He chuckled. 'Now there's an offer I've heard before. Except I think I was the one saying it, last time.' His gaze went sultry. 'And I will. Later. I'm going to kiss you all over, from the top of your head down to your toes. Your insteps. The curve of your elbow. Your navel. I'm going to explore you until you're so wet for me, so ready. And then…'

She was already wet for him. Ready. Wanting him. If he ripped her clothes off right now and took her over the desk, she wouldn't protest. 'And then?' She could hardly get the words out.

The corners of his mouth lifted in a slow, sexy smile. 'Wait and see.'

'Isn't there a saying about it being better to travel hopefully than to arrive?'

'Oh, you're going to enjoy this particular journey. I promise.' He moistened his lower lip. 'And so am I.' He paused. 'I was thinking, maybe we could go to The Green Man for dinner tonight.'

'You'll be lucky,' Alicia said. 'You have to book for weeks in advance to get a table there on Saturday nights.'

'Do you, now?' He raised an eyebrow. 'That sounds like a challenge. Have you finished plugging everything back into your computer?' At her nod, he continued, 'Then you can have first shower. Put your glad rags on. And I'll see what I can do.'

She was pretty sure he wouldn't get a table. But when she returned downstairs, showered and wearing a little black dress she hadn't worn in years, she discovered that Jack had done something even more unusual than getting a table at Paddy's.

'He's doing us a take-away?' She stared at him, utterly dumbfounded. 'But he *never* does that. Not for anyone.'

Jack shrugged. 'There's always a first time. I'm going to have a shower, then I'm going to drive down and pick up our food.'

'So you've already chosen for me?'

'Stop panicking. I'm not being a control freak. You told me that everything on the menu is fantastic—and I didn't want to wait for you to choose something, in case it gave Paddy an excuse to change his mind. So just humour me, will you?' He smiled. 'If you really want to do something, you could lay the table. And, by the way, you look delectable in that dress.'

'Thank you.'

He walked over towards her, and her heart began to beat faster. Keeping his eyes firmly fixed on hers, he placed the tip of his forefinger on her chin and slowly drew a path down her throat into the vee of her breasts, his touch so light it was barely there. 'And there's something even better than that dress. The anticipation of taking it off you. Very, very slowly,' he said, his voice husky.

He'd got her so off balance that she was all fingers and thumbs, and it took her ages to lay the table. She was faintly surprised to discover that he had a full canteen of cutlery, but she noticed that he didn't have any candles in the kitchen. And she really thought their first dinner together merited a candle. She fetched one from one of her boxes in the dining room, and set it between the two places.

When Jack came downstairs after his shower, he was wearing a white open-necked shirt and formal black trousers, and he looked stunning. Especially as he'd shaved. Unable to resist, she walked over to him and placed her fingertips against his cheek. Soft and smooth and very, very sexy. And he wasn't as cool and detached as he was trying to make out, she thought, because his pupils went huge when she touched him.

'I'll be back in ten minutes,' he said. 'You could open a bottle of red wine and let it breathe. If you like red wine?'

She didn't drink a lot, but she enjoyed the occasional glass with friends. 'Sure.'

'Pick what you want from the rack,' he said, gesturing to the small chrome rack containing half a dozen bottles of wine. 'I haven't done anything with the cellar, yet.'

But just when she thought he was about to leave, he yanked her to him and covered her mouth with his own. A slow, deep, open-mouthed kiss that left her knees weak.

'That's a down payment,' he told her, his voice husky.

Because tonight, he was going to pay up. On all of his promises.

CHAPTER NINE

ALICIA had opened a bottle of Margaux, setting it aside to breathe, and she'd just finished feeding Saffy when she heard tyres crunching on the gravel outside. A moment later, Jack walked into the kitchen with a box. 'Dinner, my lady, is served.' he said with a smile.

She'd already put two plates to warm in the oven; she retrieved them and a serving spoon, and Jack dished up.

Beef stroganoff on a bed of fluffy rice, served with *mélange* of steamed vegetables. He'd made a good choice she thought.

He clearly thought the same about her own choice, because he nodded in approval when he looked at the label. 'My favourite.' He poured them both a glass of wine while she carried the plates over to the table and lit the candle she'd placed in the middle of the table.

'To us,' he said softly, raising his glass.

'To us,' she echoed.

'You know, you really ought to be wearing diamonds,' he said.

She smiled wryly. 'No can do. They went with my mother.'

He winced. 'Sorry. I didn't intend to dredge up bad memories for you. It's just…I have these pictures in my head.'

She had a pretty good idea what kind of pictures. The same

kind of pictures that were in her own head, where he was concerned. But she asked anyway. 'Such as?'

His eyes looked very dark. And his voice had deepened when he told her, 'I have all sorts of fantasies about you. You, naked and wearing only a pair of high heels and a diamond necklace is one of them.'

She dragged in a breath. 'I'm really not a jewellery person.' She only ever wore a watch.

'I noticed.' His mouth quirked. 'You'd rather have delphiniums than diamonds.'

She inclined her head. 'Precisely.'

'You'd look fantastic naked on a bed full of delphinium petals,' he remarked. 'They'd make a nice contrast against your skin. So fair.'

Naked on a bed of scented petals.

Oh, God.

Jack Goddard had an inventive imagination. And she wasn't sure she was going to be able to live up to it.

'What about the high heels?' he asked.

She owned one pair. They were as old as the dress, and had been worn just as infrequently. And she happened to be wearing them right now. She lifted an eyebrow, keeping her gazed fixed on his. 'Take a look under the table.'

He did. And he gave a very gratifying murmur of desire when he realised that she was indeed wearing high heels. 'That'll do nicely,' he said. 'Ver-r-r-y nicely.'

The stroganoff was gorgeous, but she could barely taste it; all her senses were focused on Jack. They ate in silence, but all the way through their meal he was telling her with his eyes exactly what he wanted to do to her, and she found that breathing was difficult enough, let alone finishing her food.

He'd eaten about half of his meal when he laid down his fork and leaned back against his chair.

'What's the matter?' she asked. 'Don't you like the food?'

'It's fine.'

'Not hungry?'

'I'm hungry, all right.' His gaze met hers. 'But not for food.' The pause stretched out. And then he said softly, 'I'm hungry for you. Two days, Lissy. It's been two whole days.'

Yeah. She knew that. She'd felt every single second of them.

He moistened his lower lip with the tip of his tongue. 'And I'm *starving*.'

In answer, she stood up, blew out the candle and held out her hand.

'Now?' he asked.

She nodded.

His smile was the most sensual, most exciting thing she had ever seen.

He reached out to take her hand, and together they walked up the stairs to his room. Not only did it have a view of the lake, it contained a four-poster bed.

'I'm planning to change the hangings,' he told her. 'I was thinking of a rich, deep blue velvet spangled with stars.'

She laughed. 'You're like one of these glamorous rock stars at heart, aren't you?'

He grinned back. 'Maybe. But I've got something more important on my mind right now. You.' The pressure of his hand against hers tightened slightly, and then he let her go while he lit a candle in a wrought-iron holder and placed it on the table next to the bed. As the heat from the flame began to melt the wax, she could smell the scent of beeswax mingled with lavender.

'Now,' he said. 'I think we've both been waiting way too long for this.'

It didn't bother her that he hadn't drawn the curtains; the nearest neighbour was miles away, and nobody could see into the room. Right here, right now, it was just the two of them.

His mouth touched hers in the lightest, sweetest kiss. Then he slid one hand around the nape of her neck, underneath her hair, and found the tab of her zip. Slowly, slowly, he drew it down, the metal teeth of the zip hissing softly as they opened. Alicia could feel cool air against her back, and it made her shiver.

'Cold?' His voice was husky. 'I promise you, you're not going to feel cold soon.' He eased the material off her shoulders, and the dress fell to the floor.

'Beautiful,' he whispered, and dipped his head to press a kiss between her breasts.

She closed her eyes and tipped her head back, offering her throat to him. Slowly, his mouth traced a path upwards, skating across the hollows of her collar-bones, and then he pressed hot, open-mouthed kisses all the way up her throat. His mouth drifted round to her ear. 'I want you.'

It was mutual. But the touch of his mouth had rendered her temporarily inarticulate. She just about managed to mutter, 'Me, too.'

'I'm in your hands,' he whispered.

With shaking hands, she reached up to the first button of his shirt. Fumbled with it. It seemed to take for ever, but at last she managed to undo it. The next was easier. And the next was easier still, feeling her confidence. When she'd untucked his shirt from his trousers and undone the last button, she worked on the cuffs. Then she pushed the soft white cotton from his shoulders, letting it pool to the floor next to her dress.

'Gorgeous,' she murmured, running the flat of her arms across his pectoral muscles and up to his shoulders. There was a sprinkling of dark hair on his chest, enough to be sexy but not so much as to be off-putting, and his skin was so fair, in such sharp contrast to his hair and eyes. 'You've got Celtic colouring.'

'Right now, I feel like a Celtic warrior. As if I could conquer the world. Kiss me, Lissy,' he demanded.

She didn't need telling twice. She slid her hands round his neck, pushed her fingers into his hair, drew his head down towards hers , and brushed her mouth against his.

'Call that a kiss?' he asked, raising an eyebrow.

She smiled. 'It was your idea to make it a slow burn.'

'Not all my ideas are brilliant.' He frowned. 'I really don't think that was one of my better ones. Whereas this, on the other hand…' He wrapped one arm around her waist, hauling her closer, and slid his free hand over her buttocks. He dipped his head, nibbling at her lower lip, until she opened her mouth and let him deepen the kiss.

By the time he took his mouth from hers again, they were both shaking.

He hooked his thumbs into the waistband of her underslip and eased it over the curve of her hips. She shimmied out of it, then reached for his belt. 'My turn.' But her hands were shaking too much for her to deal with the buckle.

Jack smiled, took her hands, and kissed each fingertip in turn. Then he returned to her index finger, and drew it into his mouth. All the time, his gaze was meshed with hers, telling her that later he was going to put something much more sensitive into his mouth. And suck. Until her body went up in flames.

Alicia quivered, and the sultry look in his eyes grew even hotter. 'I'm going to make this good for you,' he promised.

She believed him. But would she be able to make it good for him? After all, Gavin had told her that even the relatively inexperienced nineteen-year-old he was seeing was more of a woman than Alicia ever had been.

As if Jack sensed that her insecurities had resurfaced with a vengeance, he cupped her face with one hand, and stroked the other one all the way down her spine. 'You're lovely. An English rose,' he said softly. 'And you turn me on in a big way.'

He undid his belt and the button of his trousers, then took her hand and guided it to the tab of his zip. Do it, his eyes implored.

They'd reached the point of no return. Or maybe they'd reached that point some time ago. She drew the zip downwards and eased the garment over his hips. When the material hit the floor, he removed his trousers and socks at the same time, then stood in front of her, completely unabashed. He certainly hadn't been lying to her about turning him on; his soft jersey boxer shorts hid absolutely nothing, so his erection was clearly outlined through the material.

And he was big.

Supposing she couldn't…?

'Stop worrying,' he said softly. 'I'm not going to hurt you. Now, my turn.' He unhooked her lacy bra. Just as he had on Thursday night, he let her breasts spill into his hands. 'Two nights I've been thinking about this,' he told her, his voice husky. 'Two nights I've been remembering how you taste. How good you smell. The texture of your skin against the tip of my tongue. And I need—oh, I *need*…' He dipped his head and drew one nipple into his mouth.

As he began to suck, Alicia slid her fingers into his hair, urging him on. It felt so good; and yet, at the same time, it wasn't enough. She wanted more. So much more. She wanted him inside her.

She must have spoken the words aloud, because he released her nipple and straightened up. 'I want to be inside you, too,' he told her huskily. 'But I want to look, first.' He gave her a sexy half-smile. 'And touch. And taste.'

He dropped to a kneeling position in front of her, and her legs turned to jelly. Surely he wasn't planning to…?

'Now, I really wasn't expecting these,' he said softly, running the tip of one finger along the lacy top of her hold-up stockings.

She flushed. 'I didn't buy them. They were a present.' From

Megan, who'd given them to her one Christmas with the instructions to wear and enjoy. Not that she ever had, until tonight. She'd never really subscribed to her best friend's theory that wearing gorgeous underwear made you feel better, but right now she was beginning to think that Megan had a point. Because Jack clearly liked what she was wearing, and it gave her confidence a much-needed boost.

'A present. Mmm. And I get to unwrap it.' He leaned forward slightly and kissed the skin of her inner thigh, just above her stocking-top. Desire flickered hotly at the base of her spine, and she felt herself growing wet between the legs.

He looked up at her, his mouth curving in that oh-so-sexy smile, and slowly rolled down the stocking-top, stroking the sensitive spot at the back of her knee and the hollows of her ankle as he smoothed the stocking down her leg. She slipped her foot from her shoe so that he could remove the stocking completely; he repeated the action with her other stocking, then slid his hand between her thighs and cupped her sex. 'You feel hot,' he remarked.

Even though the barrier between his skin and hers was thin, it was way too much for her. She needed to feel his skin against hers. Needed to feel him inside her. 'Jack. I need…'

'Me, too, honey.' His pupils were absolutely huge as he looked up at her and hooked his thumbs into the sides of her knickers. 'So?'

'Yes.' The word hissed from her. If he didn't do it now, she was going to spontaneously combust.

But when he'd removed her knickers, he stood up. Without touching her. She could have screamed with frustration. Did he really have to stop now?

Though he was still wearing his boxer shorts. She needed to do something about that.

Keeping her gaze fixed on his, she hooked her thumbs into

the side of the soft jersey, copying what he had done to her. She raised an eyebrow. 'Yes?'

'Yes.' The sound was part word, part groan.

Slowly, carefully, she eased his boxer shorts down. He stepped out of them.

And then they were equal.

Naked.

'Do something for me, Lissy?' he asked.

'What?'

'You know what I was saying downstairs about the idea of you in a pair of high heels?' He moistened his lips. 'We can take a rain check on the diamonds. And the delphiniums. Though I want you naked on midnight blue velvet at some point in the future.'

And right now he wanted her naked in high heels. Well, that was doable. Really doable. She bent down and slipped her shoes back on. 'Like this?'

He sucked in a breath. 'Do you have any idea how desirable you look and how much I want you?'

'As much as I want you,' she said.

He sat on the edge of the bed. 'Then come over here.'

She'd never played the coquette before, and although she didn't really know what she was doing she acted on instinct. She slid her hands behind the nape of her neck, gathered her hair up and held it against the back of her head, and then dropped her hands and let her hair fall down again over her shoulders. She knew she'd got it right when she heard his breath hiss sharply.

She sashayed over to him, her hands on her hips. 'Like this?'

'Uh-huh. Turn round. Slowly.'

She performed a very slow pirouette. When her back was to him, he ran his finger along the length of her spine, then stroked the curve of her bottom.

'You are glorious,' he said. 'In fact, so much that…' He stood up, scooped her up into his arms, and laid her on the bed.

Gently, he removed her shoes, stroking her instep and the hollows of her ankles. She'd had no idea that that was an erogenous zone, but when Jack touched her, it made her whole body feel as if it were blooming.

His sheets were pure cotton and felt smooth and cool against her heated skin. She closed her eyes, and felt rather than saw Jack move between her thighs, placing one hand either side of her body and dipping his head to kiss her hard. And then his mouth went gentle and he kissed her eyelids, the curve of her neck, her throat, and traced a path of kisses all the way down her torso. He circled her navel with the tip of his tongue; Alicia remembered what he said about touching his mouth to her sweet spot and couldn't suppress a needy little moan.

She felt him chuckle against her skin and then he shifted lower, kissing her thighs and running his fingertips lightly against her skin. She wriggled against the sheets and his mouth paid attention to the backs of her knees and the hollows of her ankles.

'You're driving me crazy, Jack.'

'That's the idea.'

He sounded much cooler and calmer than she felt so, not wanting to embarrass herself, she refused to open her eyes and look at him. And then, just when she didn't expect it, he slid the palms of his hands along her thighs, parting them a little more. She felt his breath whispering against her skin. And then he drew the tip of his tongue along the length of her sex.

Her breath hitched, and she almost came just from that, but then his tongue was circling her clitoris and he was easing one finger into her. Her whole body started to quiver.

'Come for me, Lissy,' he whispered.

'Oh-h-h.' She did, little shocks of pleasure rippling from deep inside and growing stronger with every wave.

When her climax had played itself out, she opened her eyes. 'My God. I never knew it could be like this.'

He raised an eyebrow. 'Are you telling me the sleazebag never made you come?'

'No-o. I mean, yes, he did. But...' she felt heat sweep into her face '...not like that.'

'You're very good for my ego.' He brushed his mouth lightly against hers, and she could taste herself on his lips. 'But I haven't finished yet. I made you a promise.' His gaze was sultry. 'To make you come again and again. And that's exactly what I'm going to do.' He opened the drawer in the table next to the bed, took a condom out of a box, removed it from the foil and slid it onto his erection.

'And as I believe in equality...' He leaned over to kiss her, then rolled onto his back, pulling her on top of him. She straddled him, and he slowly eased into her, filling her. She could hardly believe that she was aroused again so quickly; it had never been like this with Gavin. And Gavin had certainly never put her pleasure before his own.

Experimentally, she tightened her internal muscles around him, and he smiled. 'I like that. And I've got a hell of a view from here, Lissy. Have I told you yet that your breasts are perfect? And with your hair loose like that, falling down over your breasts, you look like Lady Godiva.'

'There aren't any titles in my family.'

He smiled. 'You still look like a princess. A rebel princess, one who's a bad girl at heart.'

And right now, that was exactly how she felt. Gorgeous, sexy and vibrant. Because of him.

He gripped her buttocks and tilted his pelvis, so that he could thrust more deeply inside her, and Alicia was shocked to discover the little ripples of pleasure starting again, crashing into each other and growing stronger. She'd never orgasmed a second time before, let alone as quickly as this.

Jack Goddard was one incredible man.

Just as she felt her body tightening round his he groaned her name and laced his fingers very tightly through hers. She felt his body surge against hers; then he pulled her down against him and wrapped his arms tightly round her, holding her close.

They stayed like that for a long, long time. And even though Alicia was starting to get a little cold, she didn't want to move. Ever. But, eventually, Jack dropped a kiss on the top of her head and moved her gently onto the bed. Covered her with a sheet.

'I just need to deal with the condom,' he said. 'Back in a minute.'

He was more than a minute in the bathroom. And Alicia was starting to worry that it hadn't been as good for him as it had for her when he walked into the bedroom, carrying a tub of ice cream and a spoon.

Just what she'd fantasised about, when she'd taken a peek inside his freezer.

'We didn't eat much dinner. I'm hungry now.' The corners of his eyes crinkled. 'I've done a lot of hard work.'

'I guess so,' she deadpanned. 'Are you planning to share that?'

'You like chocolate ice cream?'

She smiled. 'What do you think?'

He slid into bed beside her. 'I think my sheets could get very messy.'

Oh, the pictures *that* put in her head.

'So was it good for you?'

'You really have to ask?' She looked straight into his eyes. He wasn't fishing for compliments. He really wanted to be sure he'd pleased her. And that in itself made a funny warm feeling blossom in the region of her heart. 'Yes, it was good. Thank you. I, um…' Well, she could hardly be modest and un-assuming now. She was naked and in the man's bed. 'It's never been that good for me before.'

'I told you it wasn't *you*.' He smiled and stroked her cheek.

'And this was our first time. Imagine how good this is going to be once we've had a bit of practice.' He took a spoonful of ice cream, gave her a wicked grin—and let the dessert slide between her breasts.

She shrieked at the unexpected cold.

'Whoops. How clumsy of me. Let me deal with that,' he said, and bent his head again.

CHAPTER TEN

THE next morning, Alicia woke to find her face pillowed on a hard chest. Jack's. Even though she'd expected to sleep alone in her own room last night, he'd had other ideas. 'Stay with me tonight,' he'd said. And how could she resist those sensual blue eyes?

It had been a long, long time since she'd last spent the entire night with anyone. After sex, Gavin had always turned away from her and gone to sleep. Jack was very, very different. Quite apart from the fact that they needed a shower when they'd finished the ice cream—a shower he'd insisted on sharing, and he'd made love to her again underneath the falling spray—he'd held her close afterwards, stroked her hair, talked to her. Cuddled her to sleep.

She'd lost count of how many times they'd made love during the night. And despite the fact that she'd had nowhere near enough sleep, right at that moment Alicia felt warm and fulfilled and on top of the world. Even though muscles ached in places she hadn't even known she had, she couldn't remember ever feeling this good.

Jack was still asleep. He was actually smiling in his sleep, and he looked incredibly cute. She just about managed to resist the temptation to wake him up and wish him good morning in a very intimate way. *Later*, she promised herself. There wasn't a clock on his bedside table, so she had no idea what the time was, but she could tell from the light in the room that it was getting on for the middle of the morning. And there was something she really needed to do.

Softly, she pressed a kiss against his chest and wriggled out of his arms without waking him. She scooped up her discarded clothes and picked up her shoes, then walked barefoot to her own room to collect her dressing gown and belted it round her.

When Alicia walked into the kitchen, Saffy was delighted to see her. 'Shh,' she warned softly, and let the dog out. The table was just as she and Jack had left it, the previous night— when they'd been so hungry for each other that they hadn't even finished their meal. While the kettle boiled, Alicia scraped the leftovers into the bin, poured the rest of the wine down the sink, then stacked the crockery and cutlery in to the ancient dishwasher before making two mugs of coffee. She brought the dog back in, closed the kitchen door behind her, then carried the coffee upstairs.

Jack was just stirring when she walked into his bedroom. He opened his eyes, then sat up and stretched, looking sexily rumpled. 'Hey,' he said softly, when he saw her. 'I wasn't dreaming at all. You *are* an angel.'

'Hardly.'

'Course you are. You brought me coffee. Just the way I like it.' He smiled. 'That's a pretty dressing gown,' he observed. He beckoned to her, and she set the coffee down on the bedside table before walking over to his side of the bed. 'Nice wrapping.' His smile turned wolfish. He tugged at the belt, and the half-bow fell apart. 'Mmm,' he said, using the end of the belt to pull her nearer. He nuzzled between her breasts. 'You smell nice. I hope you don't mind your coffee cold…'

By the time he finished making love with her, the coffee was indeed cold. 'I'll make some fresh,' he said, and got out of bed in one lithe movement. He didn't bother to put any clothes on; he simply walked towards the door, naked and unashamed.

Alicia leaned back against the pillows, enjoying the view. Jack Goddard had one of the nicest backsides she'd had the privilege of seeing. 'You'd make a fabulous garden sculpture,' she said.

He turned round to look at her and his eyes danced with mischief. 'Is that a dare? Do you know anyone who does sculpture?'

'No! And, no, I don't know anyone who sculpts.' She smiled back. 'Don't tell me you're thinking about having naked statues of yourself dotted around the garden?'

He came back to sit on the edge of the bed and stroked her face. 'No, not a statue.' He stole a kiss. 'I was thinking in the flesh. Because I've still got this fantasy of making love to you in the moonlight next to the lake.'

'What about the gnats?' she asked. 'You'll be covered in bites.'

He laughed. 'Stop being so practical. Though if you insist I'll invest in some citronella candles to keep the bugs away.'

She was still smiling when he returned with more coffee and a pile of hot buttered toast. And apart from getting up to take Saffy out for a walk in the middle of the afternoon—a walk by the lake, where Jack told Alicia exactly what he intended to do there with her, one moonlit night—they spent the day in bed. Touching, tasting, exploring each other. By the evening, she'd learned exactly what would make Jack's eyes go wide with pleasure, and he'd discovered erogenous zones she hadn't even known she had.

Life, she thought, didn't get any better than this.

On Monday morning, Alicia woke up at her usual time. Jack was still asleep. She had no idea what time the builders were coming, but she decided to let him sleep in a bit longer. She'd bring him a cup of coffee in bed before she went to work—but she'd also make quite sure that she was fully dressed.

Otherwise, she knew exactly what would happen: she'd fall back into bed with him, and end up being late for work.

She showered and changed into her work clothing in her own room. But when she went downstairs to let the dog out and make breakfast, Jack was already there. He was wearing a pair of faded jeans and nothing else; he was still barefoot and he looked absolutely incredible. For a moment, she was tempted to forget work and drag him back to bed. But then common sense took over. This was a temporary affair. When it was over, she'd need places in her life that were secure. Safe. Like her job.

'Good morning,' he said. 'I've already let Saffy out. The toast should be ready in about thirty seconds or so. Have a seat.' He gestured to the table, which he'd already laid for breakfast.

'Thanks,' she said, taking a seat. This felt weird; it was the first time for a long time that she'd breakfasted with anyone. Not that she counted yesterday, as they hadn't actually *had* breakfast. 'You were sound asleep when I got up. I tried not to wake you.'

He smiled. 'I admit that I sleep in a lot later here than I do in London, but I'm used to being up early.'

'We didn't exactly have an early night.'

He raised an eyebrow. 'I burn the candle at both ends, honey.'

She couldn't suppress a self-satisfied smile. 'So I'd noticed.'

He brought over a plate of toast and sat opposite her. 'What time will you be back tonight?' he asked.

'It depends if a student wants me to go through something.' She shrugged, buttering a slice of toast. 'Probably by six. Why?'

'I thought I'd cook for us.'

She shook her head. 'You don't have to cook for me.'

'Look, it makes sense for us to eat together—what's the point in us both cooking for one?' he asked. 'Besides, it'd be using twice as much energy if we cooked separately. Not that I care about the cost to me, but I do care about the cost to the environment. So let's reduce our mutual carbon footprint.'

It was an argument she couldn't fault. 'OK.'

'I'll cook for you tonight, and you can cook for me tomorrow,' he said. 'Anything you really can't eat?'

She shook her head. 'I'm not fussy, though I'm not wonderfully keen on shellfish.'

'Noted.' He took a swig of his coffee. 'So what does Saffy do when you're at work?'

'She comes to the college with me. She sits in my office during tutorials, and comes with me if I'm in the lecture theatre. And at break time she tries to scrounge as many biscuits as she can from anyone who'll make a fuss of her.'

He laughed. 'It's nice that you can take your dog with you. If I'd taken a dog into the office, even on national Take Your Dog to Work Day, there would have been ructions.'

'So what are you doing today?' she asked.

'I've got a meeting with the builders at ten to discuss options on the stable block, the electricians are going to start work on Ted's flat, and I've got a few calls booked in with producers.' He spread honey on his toast. 'Plus I need to get supplies, as I'm cooking. Anything you need from the village?'

This felt oddly domesticated. Far more so than it had with Gavin. Then again, she hadn't been living with Gavin, except at weekends. Whereas right now she was sharing Jack's home and his bed. And although they'd agreed it wasn't a relationship, they were being honest with each other. Gavin, despite the fact he'd been engaged to her, hadn't been honest at all. She smiled at Jack. 'I'm fine, but thanks for asking.' She glanced at her watch. 'And I have to go. See you tonight.'

She sang in the car all the way to work and enjoyed every second of her lectures and tutorials. But better still was driving home to Jack. By the time she got back, the builders and the electricians had left; the only vehicle parked on the gravel was Jack's low-slung convertible. She was spared the dilemma of ringing the doorbell or using her key when the front door opened and Jack greeted her with a kiss.

'Hello, beautiful. Had a good day?' he asked.

'Fine, thanks. How did you get on with the builders and electricians?'

He smiled. 'Everything's going to plan.'

'Something smells fantastic,' she remarked as they headed for the kitchen.

'I thought I'd do us Thai food.'

It turned out to be a yellow vegetable curry, lovely little spring rolls, which Jack admitted he didn't make himself, and sticky jasmine rice. Apart from the evenings when she'd gone over to Megan's, Alicia couldn't remember the last time anyone had cooked for her. The only thing that didn't surprise her was how good it was; Jack was the type of man who'd be good at just about anything he tried to do. 'This is gorgeous. Thank you.'

His eyes crinkled at the corners. 'Pleasure.' He paused. 'I've been researching this garden archaeology stuff.'

It was completely out of left field; they hadn't spoken about the garden since he'd refused to take the journal. Alicia looked at him, too surprised to say anything.

'It seems there are three options. You either redesign the garden in a style from the past, or take the freeze-frame approach of keeping the garden as it is now while conserving the historical features.' He paused. 'Or there's the third option—creative conservation, the way Jellicoe did it.'

Alicia blinked. She hadn't expected him to have even heard of Jellicoe, let alone know anything about the landscape gardener's work. 'Sir Geoffrey Jellicoe?' she queried.

'Uh-huh.'

She frowned. 'How do you know about him?'

He shrugged. 'I came across him while I was checking out some leads on the internet.'

Now that she thought about it, it wasn't that surprising. Jack Goddard was the sort of man who, if he didn't already know about something, would research it. 'So what's your conclusion?'

'This garden has a number of historical layers: the one from the original design, then the way it changed over the years.'

She nodded.

'According to the website, Jellicoe recommended you conserve the best of each and add a new layer.'

'That's exactly what I wanted to do here—to take Alicia's journal and turn the lawn back into the original formal garden.'

'I have issues with that. Not just because of where it is— but because it's too rooted in the past. Pun not intended.' He shook his head. 'Lissy, you can't live in the past.'

'I'm not intending to. I'm just recreating the garden.'

'I can see why you want to do it. It was designed by your great-great-whatever-grandmother Alicia Beresford. But things move on, Lissy.'

'In your job, don't you work from history? I know there's also the small print about past performance not being a guide to future performance, but surely…?'

He nodded. 'I know what's likely to happen in a situation because of past experience, but at the same time in fund management you have to work in the present and be aware of what's happening around you. And I think that's true of this garden. If you lock yourself away, recreating the garden as it was in the past, that's not healthy. You've got the lake here, as well as the formal garden and the vegetable garden. Things from the past So I think you should do something new. Create it from scratch Make something that's right for the house as it is now, not just repeat what the first Alicia Beresford passed on to the house.'

'It's not repeating. It's *restoring*.'

He shook his head. 'Life moves on. Things change. And the people who came after the first Alicia added something new to the gardens. Look at your dad and his rhododendrons. He developed them, added that avenue leading to the house.'

She felt sick to her stomach. 'So you're not going to let me do it.'

'No. Doing the garden isn't going to bring your family back,' he said softly.

She lifted her chin. 'I'm not stupid. I know that.'

'Then move forward, Lissy. Put something of *you* into the garden. Whatever plant you love the most—start breeding that, or whatever it is that horticulturists do with plants. Make a new garden.'

'Just not on the lawn,' she said drily, pushing her plate away and standing up. 'Well, it's your house. Your garden. Your decision.'

'Don't make me feel bad about it.'

'Whatever.' She couldn't meet his eyes. Her throat felt tight and her eyes stung.

He gave a muffled exclamation, stood up and yanked her into his arms. 'I'm not going to fight with you, Lissy. And the only way I can do that…' He lowered her mouth to hers. Kissed her until she was breathless. Kissed her a bit more. Then he pulled away. 'Whatever happens with the garden, it's not going to affect you and me. That's completely separate.'

Was it?

He sighed. 'You're determined to make me into a caveman, aren't you?' Before she realised his intentions, he picked her up in a fireman's lift, slinging her over his shoulder, and carried her up the stairs. 'Let me prove it to you…'

CHAPTER ELEVEN

As LONG as they didn't discuss the garden, things were fine. Jack showed her Megan's plans for the house, and Alicia loved what her best friend had come up with. Just the kind of designs she would have commissioned herself, had she still owned Allingford and not had the worry of all the debts hanging round her neck.

Jack had also had the piano retuned; and one evening while he was away in London Alicia sat at the piano and played the pieces she'd loved since her teens. She was so carried away with the music that she didn't realise he'd returned until she closed the lid of the piano and heard someone clapping.

She jumped, pressing a hand to her heart. 'Jack! You gave me a fright.' She looked at Saffy. 'Some guard dog *you* are,' she said wryly.

'Hey, she's doing all right, aren't you, girl?' Jack made a fuss of the Labrador. 'Don't stop, Lissy. I was enjoying that.'

'I'm not used to playing in front of other people. I only play for me.'

'Budge up, then.' Jack sat next to her on the wide piano stool. 'Remember the first time I sat here? You thought I was going to play "Chopsticks" really badly.'

'You did,' she reminded him.

He laughed. 'On purpose, and you know it. How about a

duet? You play the melody, I'll play the bass, and then we'll swap over.'

She smiled. 'I haven't done that since I was a kid.'

'Live a little.' He lifted the lid again and began to play the bass line to 'Chopsticks', then nudged her. 'Come on, woman, you'll miss your cue.'

She laughed, and began to play the melody line. She'd forgotten how much fun it was to play the piano with someone else, and by the time they'd finished playing, half an hour later, she was completely relaxed.

'I wasn't expecting you back until tomorrow,' she said.

He shrugged. 'I decided to come home early.'

For her?

And the fact he'd called Allingford 'home'…

She suppressed the little flicker of hope. This wasn't a relationship. This was a no-strings, temporary affair. The sex was fantastic but it wasn't going to last for ever. And she had to remember that and keep that barrier round her heart. If she let Jack get too close to her, if she let herself fall in love with him, it would end in tears and heartbreak. She had to keep things light. 'So how was London?' she asked.

'Fine.' He rolled his eyes. 'That's the thing about taking a sabbatical. Nobody believes you're really going to do it—and they think they can still ask you to sort out problems.'

'Do you miss it?'

'London or my job?'

'Both.'

He pulled a face. 'Sometimes I miss London. I'm used to living in a city, to having a cinema and theatres and restaurants on my doorstep.'

'Norwich isn't that far a drive from here. Twenty minutes, if it's not the rush hour.' She spread her hands. 'Maybe we could go one evening, if you want to see a play or a film or something.'

'I'd like that.' He smiled at her. 'We could play tourist for the day, go and see the sights. I'd imagine you know quite a lot about the city's history.'

'A fair bit,' she admitted.

'Then you can be my personal tour guide. And I'll pay you in kind.' His eyes glittered. 'In fact, I think I'll buy an advance ticket.' He dipped his head and caught her lower lip between his, nipping gently until she opened her mouth and allowed him to deepen the kiss. Her fingers slid into his hair, the pads of her fingertips pressing against his scalp and urging him on.

'Let's go to bed,' Jack said when he broke the kiss, standing up and pulling her to her feet. His fingers laced through hers and he gave her a sultry look.

'I thought you'd never ask,' she said with a smile, and led him upstairs.

As the weeks passed Alicia couldn't remember ever being this happy. She loved her job, she loved living at Allingford, and she loved...

No. Not love, she reminded herself. Love wasn't on the agenda. She needed to give herself some space and get that into her head. So, that night, she made the excuse of having a headache and slept in her own room.

The headache quickly became reality; the day had been unseasonably hot and the air was close. Plus the distance between her and Jack—even though she had been the one to suggest it—made her miserable.

Something had clearly upset Lissy, Jack thought, though he didn't have the faintest idea what. She'd been sending out 'hands off' signals all evening, and he was pretty sure that her headache was manufactured. Not that he'd been able to get her to admit it.

It felt strange to be here in the four-poster bed without her. He actually *missed* her, he realised in surprise.

Without her, the bed felt too wide, and he couldn't settle to working through the file of figures in front of him. Stupid. Since Erica, he'd never let any woman get to him. Never let anyone get too close. And he and Lissy had agreed that this was a no-strings affair. This wasn't a relationship. It was just getting these crazy feelings out of their systems so that life could go back to normal.

So why was he so aware of her absence?

He was still brooding when there was a crash and his bedside light went out. 'Oh, great,' he said with a grimace. The electrician had been telling him what a state the wiring was in. Although everything was pretty much done in the two flats, the main house had yet to be fixed. He really didn't need the wiring system to go wrong now. No way would Lissy let him stay in her flat. She'd suggest that he moved into Ted's flat, or something.

Then he became aware of a light at the window, and there was another crash. Maybe it wasn't the wiring, then. A storm wouldn't usually make the electricity cut out—but then again Allingford was an old house. Alicia had said the boiler was temperamental; given what the electricians had already told him, it was a fair bet that the electricity supply was just as moody.

Another flash of lightning, and another roar of thunder. Jack thought of Saffy downstairs in the kitchen. From experience, he knew that dogs tended to be very nervous of storms. And if Alicia had taken some painkillers and was sleeping through the thunder…Ah, hell, he couldn't just leave the dog downstairs, frightened and alone. He set his file of papers on the floor, climbed out of bed, pulled on a pair of boxer shorts and padded out of his room. Without a torch, it was a bit of a pain; he hadn't been here for long enough to know his way around the house in the dark yet. But he managed to find the carved banister and made his way downstairs.

When he opened the kitchen door, Saffy whimpered and pattered over the floor to him, nudging her nose into his knee. He dropped to a crouch and made a fuss of her, calming her down. 'It's all right, girl,' he said softly. 'Just a bit of thunder. Wait until I find a torch and then I'll put the radio on for you, give you a bit of noise for company.'

First things first, he needed to get some light. Out here, there were no street lights, so in the middle of the night the only light was from the stars and the moon. On a night like tonight, when the cloud cover was thick and the rain was coming down like stair-rods, he couldn't see a thing.

There was a candle in the middle of the table, he knew. But where had he put the matches?

Just as he was about to grope his way through the drawers, a beam of light sliced into the room.

'Lissy?' he asked.

She shone the torch towards him. 'What are you doing up?'

'I thought Saffy might be worried by the storm. I need to find the matches.'

'Here.' She walked over to him and handed him the torch.

'Thanks.' With the help of the beam from the torch he managed to find the matches, then lit the candle and switched off the torch. 'That's better for you, girl?' he asked the dog, who nudged his knee again and licked him. He smiled and ruffled her fur, then turned to Alicia. 'How's your headache?' he asked.

'About the same.'

'I can do something about that. Sit down,' he said. He walked over to his MP3 player, and chose a playlist that he'd made at a time when the financial markets had been going through a really rough time, and he'd needed something to relax him in the office. The soft, regular notes of a Vivaldi cello concerto floated into the air, and he went to stand behind Alicia's chair. Gently, he slid his fingers into her hair, massaging her scalp with his fingertips, using enough pressure to help ease the ache but not so much that it would make the pain worse.

'Oh-h-h, that's good. Where did you learn to do this?' she asked.

'My sister's a nurse. She taught me. Apparently stimulating the blood flow to the scalp is one of the quickest ways to get rid of a headache.'

He wanted to touch her more intimately, but he knew that now was the wrong time to push it. Even if she didn't have a headache, she'd been distant with him, and the last thing he wanted to do was to open that distance even further. At least she was letting him this close. He had to be content with that, for now.

He continued massaging her scalp until she slid her hands over his, stilling them. 'Thank you, that really helped,' she said softly.

'No problem,' he responded politely. He bent to make a fuss of the dog again, then went back over to the MP3 player and switched it over to the radio, skipping through the frequencies until he found a talk show. 'The battery should last for a few hours, at least until the storm is over. Hearing voices is going to make Saffy feel a lot less worried about the thunder,' he said. Then he turned and saw the strain on Alicia's face. Was she worried about him? Did she think he was going to pressure her, demand sex just because he helped her headache? 'Are you sure you're all right?' he asked.

'I'm fine.'

'We said, no lies,' he reminded her softly. 'Tell me what's wrong.'

She grimaced. 'I used to have recurring dreams about a tower being struck by lightning.'

'Symbolic?' Given that her family had crashed round her ears, her dreams could have reflected her emotional turmoil.

She shook her head. 'I know exactly where that one comes from. When I was a kid, one of Dad's friends had this old ruined folly in his garden. I used to play there and make up stories about princesses being rescued from towers—typical girly sort of thing—until the guy's son told me what happened there. Apparently, many years before, it was hit by lightning and the tower collapsed. He said a girl was killed in the top room of the tower, and her spirit haunted the folly.' She shivered. 'And he said that on stormy nights, her ghost came to the house and suffocated anyone who was staying in her bed.'

'And you had this girl's old room?'

'Don't you laugh at me,' she warned.

'I'm not laughing at you. Lots of people are scared of storms. And that was a really mean thing to say to a little girl.' He walked over to her and squeezed her hand. 'So what happened?'

She swallowed. 'We were staying there once when there was a storm. The thunder woke me up and I screamed the place down, convinced it was the ghost come to strangle me. And ever since then, I've dreamed about the girl and the tower being hit by lightning whenever there's been a storm.' She grimaced. 'I'm such a wuss. That's why I prefer not to watch spooky films.'

'How old were you when all this happened?'

'About eight.'

'And the boy?'

She shrugged. 'Not sure. Early teens, I guess.'

'Did your brother know about this?'

She shook her head. 'If I'd told him, Ted would've pasted him over a square mile. But the boy—I can't even remember his name, now—said if I told anyone the ghost would get me.'

'So he scared you into silence. That's…' He shook his head in disgust. 'And you've never told anyone about this?'

'Because it's stupid. Ridiculous. I know that, intellectually.'

'But emotionally it's a different matter.' He paused. He knew he probably shouldn't say this, but he really couldn't stop himself. 'You know, to overcome your fears, what you need i to associate storms with something pleasurable instead of your old nightmare.'

'Pleasurable.' Her expression turned sultry and she licked her lower lip.

God, he wanted her. He could feel his body starting to tighten with anticipation.

He lifted her hand to his mouth and pressed a kiss into her palm. 'I missed being with you tonight, Lissy.'

Her eyes looked very dark in the candlelight. She opened her mouth—he hoped, to say that she'd missed him too—but then there was another crash of thunder. Saffy whined and Lissy's face paled.

'I'll turn the radio up for the dog,' he said, 'and you need to come with me. I'm not going to leave a candle on down here because it wouldn't be safe, but we can leave the torch on for Saffy and I'll get a new battery for it tomorrow.' He released Alicia's hand, switched the torch back on and adjusted the angles so that the beam lit Saffy's corner of the kitchen. 'It'll be over soon, girl,' he reassured her. The dog climbed back into her basket and curled up with her head on her paws, looking sad.

Jack smiled wryly. He'd always been a sucker for big brown eyes. Probably part of the reason why he'd married Erica.

Not that he wanted to think about his ex-wife tonight.

He picked up the candlestick, laced his fingers through Alicia's, and led her back up the stairs to his room.

This was practically a Mr Darcy fantasy come true, Alicia thought. Walking hand in hand with Jack up the stairs at Allingford, by candlelight. All he needed were tight breeches and a white shirt with a cravat instead of his jersey boxer shorts; and for her to be wearing a Victorian long white lacy nightgown instead of a short red jersey nightdress with white polka dots and spaghetti straps…

She shivered, and his fingers tightened around hers.

'It's OK. You're perfectly safe.'

She knew he was referring to the storm; she might be safe from that, but she certainly wasn't safe from Jack Goddard.

As usual, his bedroom curtains weren't closed. She'd asked him about it before, and he'd merely laughed. 'It's refreshing to wake up and just see the sky and hear birdsong, instead of opening the blinds to look out at London and hear traffic.'

Jack placed the candle on the bedside table, then led her over to the window. 'The wide skies in Norfolk are amazing. This is where I wish we had one of those rooms with panoramic views,' he said. 'One of those cupolas with glass all round and a three-hundred-and-sixty-degree view, so we could see the storm spiralling round us.'

She shivered. 'I'm not sure I could cope with that.'

'Yes, you could, because you'd be with me,' he promised. He took her hands and placed them on the wooden glazing bars, just above the height of her head. 'Lean forward,' he said.

She did so, resting her forehead against the glass.

'Now watch,' he whispered.

A few moments later, lightning split the sky in a hard white forked line; as she watched she noticed that the dark grey sky turned the palest shade of pink radiating out from the lightning.

'Isn't it beautiful?' he asked.

Yes, but it was scary at the same time. She could feel the rumble of the thunder through the wooden bars, and she shivered. The coldness of the glass against her face was counterbalanced by the heat of Jack's body behind her; his arms were wrapped around her waist and his head was on her shoulder.

'What is it that scares you, the lightning or the thunder?' he asked.

'Both, I think.'

'OK. The thunder isn't going to hurt you, it's just a noise, and you know the old trick about counting the seconds after the lightning until you hear the thunder? Each second means the storm is a mile further away. So the lightning's not going to strike you.'

She counted under her breath as the lightning lit the sky again. 'Fifteen seconds. Fifteen miles.'

'It only looks nearer because the skies here are so wide, so beautiful. Look at the lightning—such pure whiteness streaking through the skies, such incredible energy. Look at the way it colours the air around it, pink and blue and green.'

'How does it do that?'

'No idea!' he said laughing. 'Let's just enjoy the show for now. You're perfectly safe in here with me. Nothing bad's going to happen. No towers, no ghosts. Just you and me watching a glorious storm.'

The usual tension she felt during a storm started to seep out of her. She could feel the incredible restless energy in the air and the echo of the thunder through the wood, see the blaze of light spearing through the heavens—and then there was a different sort of tension altogether. An electric tension that crackled like lightning between them.

Jack's mouth was right next to Lissy's ear, and he could smell the sweet floral scent he always associated with her. So sweet and innocent compared with the sophisticated musky scent most of the women he knew wore, and yet it turned him on. Big time.

He nuzzled her hair out of the way. Her skin was soft and warm beneath his mouth, enticing him. Slowly, he drew a trail of kisses along her shoulder, down her spine, until he reached the top of her nightdress. She arched back against him and he caught one of the spaghetti straps between his teeth and pulled it down over her shoulder. When she didn't move away, he did the same with the other strap, then gently eased the nightdress down until it pooled at her feet.

'Keep watching the lightning,' he told her huskily.

She did, and he kissed his way down her spine. 'Your skin's so soft,' he murmured. 'You smell nice. And I can't resist you.'

'Then don't.'

He smiled against her skin and continued kissing her, caressing her, until she shivered. Not from cold, he knew: from desire. The same desire that was making his own control snap. This was what he wanted her to think about, the next time she saw a storm. Not some stupid, untrue ghost story that had scared her silly: he wanted her to think of him, of his body sliding into hers and pushing deep. 'Lissy,' he whispered, 'I want you.'

'Yes.' She was still gripping the glazing bars. And in the candlelight, she looked absolutely stunning. He'd never thought about it before, but now, he really wished he could draw. He'd draw her, looking out on the rain and the lightning. sketch in the shadows cast by the candlelight. But even then, he wouldn't be able to capture the smoothness and the softness of her skin—or what it felt like to glide his hand over the curve of her perfect buttocks, the weight of her breasts in his hands, the way that sliding into her made him feel as though he'd been wrapped in warm, wet silk.

'I want to make love with you,' he said, the words coming from deep inside him. Because this wasn't just sex. And although he knew this was dangerous—way too dangerous, and he ought to stop right now because he didn't want his heart involved—he really couldn't help himself. He needed to lose himself inside her. Right now.

He took a couple of steps back, opened the drawer of his bedside table and rummaged in it until he found a condom. His hands were actually shaking when he ripped the foil packet apart and slid the latex on. And then he was standing behind her again. Resting his hands on the curve of her waist. 'Are you sure about this?'

He couldn't be completely selfish. Much as he wanted her, he wasn't going to push her into doing something she might not want to do.

'I'm sure,' she said softly.

'Keep watching the storm,' he whispered. He positioned himself at her entrance, then slowly pushed inside her. He noticed that her grip on the glazing bars grew even tighter. Yeah, that was how he felt too. Coiled up and needing release.

The storm was growing nearer, the gaps between the lightning becoming shorter. With every flash of light, he pushed deeper into her, taking it slowly. Her breath hissed, and he quickened the pace of his thrusts slightly. 'Is this helping?'

'Yes and no,' she said. 'I don't think I'm scared of storms any more. But when I close my eyes, I can still see the lightning every time you push into me.'

Lightning he was starting to see, too.

As the storm hit its peak he felt her internal muscles rippling round him, pushing him over the edge to his own climax. He wrapped his arms tightly round her, burying his face in her shoulder, and felt her shudder in his arms.

They stayed locked together there by the window until the storm had faded; then he withdrew, scooped her up and carried her over to the bed. He dealt with the condom, then curled up in bed beside her.

'Thank you,' she said softly, leaning forward and kissing the tip of his nose. 'I'm going to associate storms with something very different, now.'

Something much more pleasurable, judging by that incredibly sexy smile. He smiled back. 'Good. But I still think you should spend the rest of the night in my bed, not yours. Just in case there's another storm and you need a bit more therapy.'

And because he didn't want her to go.

Though he wasn't ready to tell her that.

And he wasn't sure if she was ready to hear it anyway.

CHAPTER TWELVE

ALTHOUGH the electricians had officially finished work on Alicia's flat, Jack persuaded her not to move back straight away.

'Saffy's settled and it's not fair to keep moving her between your flat and my house,' he said. 'Plus it's a lot easier for us to share a kitchen than for us to have separate fridges and separate ovens and so on.'

'True. But I'm dependent on you, here,' Alicia argued.

'No, you're not,' he said. 'You have your own room.' Not that she'd slept in it, since the night of the storm. 'Anyway, I don't have anyone to help me move your furniture back.'

Alicia scoffed. 'You've got three builders working on the stable block, plus the electricians. I'm sure one of them would help. Or I could get one of my colleagues to come and lend a hand.'

No, no, no. That wasn't what he wanted. He changed tack. 'OK. Suppose you move back to your flat. You have a double bed. Which isn't as comfortable as a king size.'

She had to admit that.

'And do you really want to mess about every night, making sure you've locked up and brought Saffy's bed over? It'd be *much* easier for you to stay here.'

'Are you asking me to move in with you?'

Yes. No. He frowned. 'We're just continuing an arrangement that suits us both. Making life easy.'

'Hmm.'

'And besides,' he added, 'if you stay here, you can see how Meg's designs are shaping up.' The decorators were transforming one room at a time, and so far he loved what they'd done. Kept the spirit of the house and yet brought it into the present.

'We're not having a relationship,' she reminded him.

'Course not.' He smiled. 'This is what we agreed to. Hot, no-strings sex. Speaking of which…'

One Wednesday morning, Jack persuaded Alicia to spend the afternoon with him in the city. 'If I do the lawn this morning, then that gives you a free afternoon—because you don't have to worry that the lawn's going to grow wildly out of control between mowings. And I'd like to walk round Norwich with someone who knows it.'

'OK,' she agreed with a smile.

'And I might as well drop you off at work,' he continued. 'Otherwise, you'll have to come back here first, and then you'll be doubling back on yourself. And it's senseless us taking separate cars.'

'What about Saffy?' Alicia asked.

'If you don't mind, you could leave her here with me for the morning. I can take her for a run before I do the mowing. You'll be all right with me, won't you, girl?' he asked the dog.

The Labrador thumped her tail and plonked her teddy bear on his knee.

'It's all right by her, if it's all right by you,' he told Alicia with a smile.

'No feeding her chocolate biscuits,' Alicia warned. 'It's really bad for her teeth.'

'Scouts' honour,' he said.

She scoffed. 'I bet you were never a boy scout.'

'Well, no,' he admitted. 'But I hope you feel you can trust me.'

She looked at him for a long, long moment, and then she nodded. 'I do.'

He drove her to work with the hood of his car down, so her hair was a complete mess by the time he pulled up in the car park. She looked utterly delectable, and Jack couldn't resist stealing a kiss.

'Better,' he said. 'And I'll pick you up at…?'

'Half past twelve.'

'Have a nice day.' He smiled at her as she climbed out of the car. But then he noticed the curious glances from people walking past them—some of them clearly young enough to be students and others who were more likely to be her colleagues.

Hmm.

She'd worked with her sleazebag ex. And after his affair had become common knowledge, no doubt she'd been an object of pitying glances and little whispers in the staffroom.

Maybe it was time he gave them something to think about. Boosted Alicia's street cred a bit. The car was a good start, but he could think of something better.

'Lissy?' he said.

'Mmm-hmm?'

'Something I nearly forgot.'

She frowned. 'What?'

He crooked his index finger, and she walked round to his side of the car. Leaned over, just as he hoped she would. Then he slid his hand under her hair, yanked her mouth towards his and kissed her thoroughly. A long, hot, open-mouthed kiss that would leave their spectators in no doubt whatsoever about the fact that he was having hot sex—and lots of it—with Alicia Beresford. And that he thought she was the most gorgeous woman in the universe.

'Don't be late. *Ciao*, babe,' he said, blew her another kiss, and drove away, leaving her staring after him and looking stunned.

She was simmering when he picked her up at lunchtime. 'Why the hell did you kiss me like that this morning in front of everyone?' she hissed.

'Because you're gorgeous and I wanted to. Smile, people are watching,' he warned her. 'Unless, of course, you want a proper hello kiss?'

'Don't even think about it!' She climbed into the car, and did up her seat belt.

'And I thought *I* was the one who got moody when my carb levels dropped too low,' he remarked, pulling out of the car park.

'Do you have any idea how many people have been asking me about you today?' she demanded.

He shrugged. 'Let them ask.'

'I *hate* people prying into my private life.'

He reached across briefly and squeezed her hand. 'OK, I'm sorry. I got it wrong. But I noticed people were staring at us this morning, and I thought you'd probably had a hard time because of what's-his-face. Sleazebag. I just wanted to even up the balance a bit. Show them that you're not someone to feel sorry for—you're an incredibly gorgeous, sexy woman, as well as a bright, intelligent, capable lecturer.'

'Hmm.'

He sighed. 'All right. I promise not to embarrass you in future, OK? Now let's go and have lunch and a wander round the city.'

When they'd parked, she took him to a small café in one of the back streets, where they served the best coffee and chicken Caesar wrap he'd ever tasted.

'I really wasn't expecting this,' he admitted.

'There *is* life outside London,' she said, giving him a pained look. 'And at one point Norwich was the second city of England. Second only to London—and our city walls enclosed a bigger area.'

He'd already noticed that the cathedral and the castle dominated the skyline. 'I'm looking forward to exploring the place. With you.' He reached across the table and linked his fingers through hers. 'Have you forgiven me yet?'

'For kissing me stupid in front of my colleagues and students?' She smiled wryly. 'I suppose so.'

'Good. So where are you going to take me?'

'If it was a Sunday, I'd suggest taking you to the Plantation Garden. It's just on the outskirts of the city, outside the line of the old walls; it was made out of a chalk quarry by a Victorian upholsterer and cabinet-maker. It's an amazing place, with tree-ferns and palms and the most incredible Gothic fountain.'

He rolled his eyes. 'I should have guessed you'd pick a garden.'

'Norwich used to be known as the city of orchards and gardens,' she informed him. 'So I have a lot of choices. The Plantation Garden was abandoned after the war, but it was restored a few years ago.'

He had a nasty feeling he knew where this was leading.

His thoughts must have shown on his face, because she shook her head. 'It's all right. I'm not going to bend your ear about restoring the garden at Allingford. You know how I feel about it; I know how you feel about it. And it's a circular argument. It's pointless starting it all up again.'

'I don't want to fight with you today, Lissy.' He leaned forward and whispered in her ear, 'Unless you're planning on some really hot making-up sex. In which case, feel free to have all the fights with me you want.'

Gratifyingly, her face turned bright pink. He grinned and punched his fist in the air. '*Yes!* Result.'

'I hate you.'

'No, you don't. Because I'm going to buy you cake, later. Ready to start showing me round the city, then?'

She led him down a narrow cobbled street, past half-timbered houses. 'We haven't got time to do everything today,' she told him. 'So it's up to you if you want to do the river walk or have a look around the cathedral.'

He spread his hands. 'I'm the tourist. Show me the pretty bits.'

'The cathedral,' she decided. 'It's one of my favourite places—it's really peaceful. The Bishop's House Garden won't be open today, but I'll bring you next time it is. You'd never believe you were smack in the middle of the city because it's so quiet, and it hasn't changed much over the last seven hundred years. And, do you know, it actually has a hebe that was grown from a cutting from Queen Victoria's wedding bouquet?'

Trust Alicia to know something like that.

'And there are also these incredible blue Himalayan poppies…'

He was struck by how animated she looked as she talked about the plants. And the mention of the poppies triggered something in his memory. 'You really like blue flowers, don't you? I remember you said you were growing delphiniums in our garden.' And there had been a carpet of bluebells.

She nodded. 'I love delphiniums and cornflowers. And I think some of the big blue flag irises would look fantastic over by the lake.'

'Then why don't you make a blue garden at Allingford?' He slid his arm round her shoulders. 'I like the idea of that— because then you'll be giving the garden something of *you*.'

'I thought we weren't going to discuss the garden?'

'We're not. I'm just giving you something to think about.'

They wandered through the cathedral close together, and Alicia took him into the beautiful Romanesque building, showing him the carved and painted bosses on the vaulting. 'This one's my favourite—the green man,' she said.

He could really see how she'd inspire her students. She was full of knowledge, but she didn't just parrot out dry facts. She told him stories to rouse his interest, made him guess why there was a musket ball in the tomb of one of the bishops and why the mellow Caen stone had turned pink in places. And he couldn't ever remember enjoying himself more.

From the cathedral, she took him up to the castle. Pinched his backside in the dungeons when the guide turned the lights out to show them what the conditions were like for the prisoners. Got him to drop money down the castle well and count the seconds until he could see the ripples on the water in the bottom as the coin hit.

They were heading back to the car when Jack spotted something in the window of an antique shop. Something he thought would be perfect for her. Something he wanted to get her as a surprise. He waited until they'd gone further down the street and were outside a bookshop when he said, 'There's something I need to do. Can I leave you here for a minute?'

To his relief, she didn't ask questions so he didn't have to be evasive. She just smiled. 'Sure. I'll browse in here while I'm waiting for you.'

He dropped a kiss on the tip of her nose. 'I'll come and find you. Back soon.'

Alicia had no idea what Jack was up to or where he was going, but she wasn't going to pry. It was probably something to do with work. Instead, she went into the bookshop and dawdled round the shelves, picking up books that caught her eye and flicking through them.

'Alicia? Is that you?'

Her mouth went dry. She recognised that voice. And she remembered the last time he'd spoken to her. Very, very well.

She wasn't going to let him think he'd thrown her. She took her time turning to face him, and said coolly, 'Hello, Gavin.'

The man who'd broken her heart.

The man who'd convinced her that their break-up was all her fault.

The man who'd cheated on her, lied to her—and who'd made her think she was the one who was useless at sex.

'You're looking well,' he said.

She inclined her head in acknowledgement. 'How are you?'

'Fine.'

He didn't look it. There were shadows under his eyes and, she thought with a guilty surge of satisfaction, his hairline was definitely receding. In ten years' time, she'd just bet he'd be bald and paunchy.

'Cherie not with you?' she asked.

He had the grace to flush. 'No. We, um, split up a while back.'

She didn't ask for details. She really didn't want to know. 'Job going OK?'

He wrinkled his nose. 'I miss the old place.' He looked rueful. 'Actually, I miss a lot of things. I've made a lot of mistakes, Lissy. I wish…' He shook his head. 'I treated you really badly, and I'm sorry.'

'Mmm-hmm.' Oh, God. Please don't let him say he wanted her back.

No way.

Even if she hadn't been involved in the relationship-that-wasn't-a-relationship with Jack, she wouldn't go back to Gavin now. She'd moved on. You couldn't change the past.

'I was wondering…'

Just at that moment, an arm slid possessively round her shoulders and she felt a kiss in the sensitive spot beside her ear. 'Sorry I was a while, honey,' Jack said. 'Did I keep you waiting very long?'

Nope. He'd come to the rescue at the perfect time. She gave him a grateful look. 'No, it's fine.'

He obviously interpreted her expression as a signal to kiss her on the mouth. Hard and deep, leaving her breathless.

And when Jack broke the kiss, Alicia was secretly delighted to see how uncomfortable Gavin looked.

So she was rubbish at sex, was she? Didn't respond properly, didn't know how to turn a man on?

'Sorry. I didn't realise…' Gavin began.

'Of course you wouldn't. Jack, this is Gavin Lawson,' she said. 'Gavin, this is Jack Goddard.'

Jack held his hand out to Gavin, and clearly his handshake was extremely firm because Gavin actually winced.

'So you and Alicia are…' Gavin's voice tailed off.

'I believe the usual euphemism is "just good friends",' Jack said with a smile. He rested his cheek against Alicia's hair. 'You're a colleague?'

'Used to be.' Gavin lifted his chin. 'Actually we were more than that. Alicia was my fiancée.'

'Oh?' Jack sounded bored. 'Oh, well. Your loss. But definitely my gain. Did you find anything you wanted, honey?' he asked Alicia.

She shook her head. 'I was just browsing.'

'We really ought to make a move. Otherwise we're going to be late for dinner.'

'It's only just gone five,' Gavin said pointedly.

Jack smiled. 'I know. But by the time we've had a shower together, it'll be more like seven.'

Alicia stared in surprise as a dull tide of colour washed over Gavin's face. She'd never, ever seen him embarrassed before.

'Nice to meet you,' Jack said, his tone saccharine-sweet. 'Ready, honey?' And with that he swept her out of the shop. Out of Gavin's reach.

He didn't mention a word about Gavin on the way home. Or what his mysterious errand was. But when they'd had dinner, he said softly, 'Are you all right?'

She frowned. 'Yes. Why?'

'Seeing Gavin again must have brought back a lot of memories.'

'A bit.' She paused. 'He told me he'd split up with Cherie. The girl he left me for.'

Jack waited a beat. 'Do you want to cool it between us?'

'Do you?' she fenced, her stomach suddenly feeling hollow. What was this all about? Was this Jack's way of letting her down gently, now it was over?

'I was just wondering. Now you've seen him again, now he's free…do you want him back?'

She shook her head emphatically. 'I'd never be able to trust him again. And trust is important in a relationship.'

His face was suddenly unreadable.

Because she'd said the R-word.

'So are you looking for this thing between us to be something more?' he asked.

She couldn't tell a thing from his tone. Did he want to move their affair on to the next level? Or would saying 'yes' be the quickest way to make him leave her?

'I'm fine with hot sex and no strings,' she said, trying to keep her own voice as neutral as possible. 'I'm not bored…yet.'

He grinned. 'I should hope not.' Then he sobered. 'I enjoyed today. Walking and talking with you. I just wanted you to know that I…like you.'

Jack had been hurt before. According to Jimmy, Erica had broken Jack's heart. Was this his way of telling her he wanted to try to make a go of things with her, but 'like' was the best he could offer?

Or was he trying to let her down gently?

Or was this his way of making a declaration?

She had no idea. Couldn't read what was going on in his head. Couldn't even begin to guess. So she played it safe. 'I had a nice time, too.'

'Good. Let's go to bed.'

Though when she lay back against the pillows, she could feel something lumpy. 'Hang on. I need to sort this out.' She grasped the pillow, intending to fluff it up, and discovered something hard beneath her fingers. 'What's this?' she said, taking it out. A blue box, wrapped with a pale blue ribbon with curled edges.

'What does it say on the label?' he asked.

A pale blue star, matching the ribbon exactly. 'My name,' she said, frowning.

He shrugged. 'Then I guess it's for you.'

She undid the ribbon carefully, and stared in surprise as she opened the box. It contained a pendant, a stylised art deco iris enamelled on silver. 'It's beautiful,' she said, touching it reverently.

'I know you're not a jewellery person,' he said, 'but it caught my eye and made me think of you. That blue's the same colour as your eyes. I wanted to surprise you—that's why I asked you to wait for me in the bookshop.'

She couldn't remember the last time anyone had ever bought her jewellery—apart from her watch, which had been a twenty-first present from her father and Ted. And this was special. Not only was it precious in its own right, he'd bought it with her in mind. Because of the blue flowers.

'Thank you. It's gorgeous. Would you…?' She held the box out to him, and when he took it from her she turned her back to him.

He put the necklace on for her, dealing with the clasp, then turned her round to face him. 'Not diamonds,' he said, 'or even delphiniums.'

But a blue flower. One of her favourites. One she'd told him she wanted to plant round the lake. Something that might be part of a blue garden. 'It's perfect, Jack. Thank you.'

* * *

She liked it. She really liked it—she wasn't just being polite or trying to spare his feelings. She was actually blinking away tears.

'Don't cry.'

'I'm not. Eyelash.'

It was a fib, and both of them knew it.

He made love to her slowly, that night. Slowly and very, very thoroughly—and he made sure that when she climaxed her eyes were open and she was seeing him. That she called *his* name.

It shocked him that he'd actually felt jealous in the bookshop; after all, what possible reason would Alicia have for going back to the man who'd hurt her and humiliated her?

Not that he and Alicia were having a proper relationship anyway.

It was just that the incident had stirred up his memories of Erica, the way she'd let him down so badly. He'd promised himself back then that he'd never, ever put himself in that position again, and nothing had changed.

He'd bought Alicia a necklace, not a wedding ring.

No strings.

Afterwards, she lay with her head on his shoulder.

'I've got more hair than he has, you know,' Jack said.

She chuckled. 'You've got more of a lot of things than he has.'

'Oh? That sounds interesting.'

'Stop fishing.' She tapped his wrist. 'But you are much better in bed than he was.'

'And so are you,' he said. 'I think he was trying to cover up for his own inabilities. And he conned you into thinking it was your fault.' He paused. 'So you don't work together any more?'

'No. And he didn't live in the village, so at least I was spared that.' She paused. 'Though I've bumped into his mother a few times. It was a bit embarrassing.'

'For her or for you?'

'For both of us,' Alicia admitted wryly. 'She was all right, but I think I probably had a lucky escape. She's one of these women who would have dropped in at every possible opportunity and driven me crazy with her advice about how to do things. Well meaning but very, very interfering.'

'I'm glad my mother isn't like that,' Jack said thoughtfully. 'She thought I was mad, buying somewhere outside London, but she's given me space.' He paused. 'Though I think I'm going to have to invite my family down here. I'm getting some very sarcastic texts from my sister.'

'Didn't Jimmy fill her in?'

'Apparently not. She wants to know what I'm hiding.'

'It's your house. It's up to you what to do.' She paused. 'Do you want me to be out of the way for their visit?'

Uh-oh. Was it that obvious? And was it a problem for her? 'Why would I want that?' he asked, hoping to sidestep the issue.

She flushed. 'Well, the situation between you and me…'

'Is our business and nobody else's,' he finished. He kissed her lightly. 'We're fine as we are. Stop worrying.'

But all the same, he slept badly that night.

If he let his family meet Lissy…things would change. Because then it would stop being hot sex with no strings. His family would start having expectations. Drop hints about what a nice girl Lissy was and how she seemed good for him. In fact, knowing Cathy, she'd say straight out that it was time he got over Erica and married again.

Which wasn't what he wanted. He'd been there, done that, and knew marriage wasn't for him. And he liked things just the way they were.

So he'd make some excuse to keep the real world away a little longer.

CHAPTER THIRTEEN

'You,' Megan said, 'look fantastic.'

'Glowing skin, shiny hair…and for the first time since I can remember she doesn't look worried. Good sex obviously agrees with her,' Grace said with a broad smile. 'So come on, Lissy. Admit it. We were right, weren't we?'

Alicia felt her face turn bright red. 'Do you mind? I'm not discussing my private life.'

'Just as well you didn't take that bet with me.' Grace raised an eyebrow. 'Have you actually spent a night in your own bed, without him, in the past month?'

'I'm not discussing this,' Alicia said through gritted teeth.

'She hasn't,' Grace informed Megan in a stage whisper.

'And you would know because, as Jack's part-time housekeeper, you make the beds and do the laundry,' Megan replied, also in a stage whisper.

Alicia groaned. 'Oh, for goodness' sake! You two are impossible!'

'So it's serious, then?' Megan asked.

'No, it's not. We're not having a relationship. We're just…' Alicia flapped a dismissive hand. 'Look, we're young, free and single—and, since you want to know the gory details, yes, we fancy the pants off each other, and we're enjoying having sex with each other.'

'Lots of it,' Grace added with a wink.

Then Megan's smile dissolved into concern. 'Lissy, you do know what you're doing, don't you?'

'Course I do,' Alicia replied breezily, lying through her teeth. 'Taking the advice you two gave me and having hot sex with a gorgeous man.' Sitting in Megan's living room with her best friend and Grace, while Megan's three-year-old daughter Jenny was having an afternoon nap and there was nobody to overhear them, was about the only time and place she'd have this sort of conversation.

'Jack's gorgeous, and he's a nice guy—but he's not going to settle here for ever,' Megan warned.

'He's a city boy,' Alicia said. 'Of course he's going to go back to London. I wouldn't expect anything else. And I'm not planning to go back to London with him—so when it's over, it's over.' She shrugged. 'I've got my eyes wide open and my feet on the ground. I know what I'm doing. There's nothing to worry about.'

Though Megan had unconsciously echoed the little voice Alicia had refused to let herself listen to. The little voice that told her she was falling in love with Jack Goddard. The sex was amazing, but it was more than just physical gratification. She liked being with Jack. Liked fencing verbally with him, liked messing about on the piano with him, liked taking Saffy for a run with him. Liked showing him the little bits she loved in her part of the world—the endless sandy beach on the north Norfolk coast, wall paintings and misericords in tiny round-towered churches, poppies bursting round the edges of the cornfields, the stunning gardens in the local stately homes.

Oh, Lord.

They'd agreed up front that this was just sex.

And she needed to remember that.

Her worries deepened when Jack finally arranged for his family to come to Allingford and give the place the once-over. Because when she repeated her earlier suggestion of being out of the way when they arrived, Jack looked relieved. 'Do you mind?'

'No. There are a couple of gardens I want to see—they're only open a couple of weekends a year and this weekend happens to be one of them.'

But all the same, it hurt.

Because it underlined the fact that this was only temporary for him. He didn't want her to meet his family—because meeting family was what happened when you took your relationship to the next level. And they'd agreed they weren't having a relationship anyway.

Although Alicia pretended everything was fine, by Sunday morning she was a nervous wreck. She was awake really early, practically before the dawn chorus had started, and, although part of her was tempted to wake Jack up and make love with him to wipe the worries out of her mind, she couldn't be that selfish. Instead, she left him to sleep and slipped quietly out of bed. She had a quick shower, pulled on her gardening clothes, sorted out some things in the kitchen and then headed for the garden with the dog, warning Saffy to be quiet and not to bounce about over the lawn, barking at sparrows the way she usually did.

There was only one way to get rid of this nervous energy.

And it involved digging up nettles.

Three hours later, Jack appeared with two mugs of coffee and handed one to her. 'The bed is freezing cold, so I assume you've been out here for hours.'

She wasn't going to admit to the real reason why. 'Weeds don't stop growing, you know. Especially when we've had the amount of rain we've had this week. They need to be removed before they get too big and start seeding.'

He wasn't fooled for a moment. 'I know this is the way you deal with things. You go into the garden and work out your worries on the weeds. But stop fretting. Everything's going to be fine.' He leaned over and kissed the tip of her nose. 'And thanks for preparing the veg for Sunday lunch. You really didn't have to do that.'

Especially because she wasn't actually staying for lunch.

She shrugged. 'I don't mind. Anyway, I thought your family might like to have home-grown organic veg from your country estate. I dug up some extra in case they wanted to take some home with them.' She took a swig of the coffee. 'Thanks for the coffee. I'll be out of your way in half an hour.'

'You don't have to go yet. They're going to call me when they turn off the A11—twenty minutes away. Which means we have ages.' He gave her a sultry look. 'Come back to bed.'

Alicia was tempted. But at the same time she was very aware of the fact he didn't want her to meet his family. And that had started to rankle. So she gave him a sweet smile and shook her head. 'Later. These weeds aren't going to sort themselves.'

'I suppose. I'll see you later, then,' he said and kissed her lightly.

She smiled back and pretended everything was fine, but she didn't believe him.

Because this felt like the beginning of the end.

Jack's family hadn't called by the time Alicia came back in to shower and change. And he was giving her a long, slow, leisurely kiss goodbye in the hall when Saffy barked.

They sprang apart.

'It can't be,' Jack said, his eyes widening. 'They haven't phoned me yet.'

But there was the faint crunch of gravel, and then the doorbell went.

Oh, no.

And she couldn't even creep out the back way—her car was

parked next to Jack's and it would be way, way too obvious if she left. Rude. And she'd always been brought up to be polite.

She could see similar thoughts in his eyes.

'Well, I suppose as you're here—' he began.

'I'll say hello and make a fast exit.'

Jack opened the front door. 'Mum! I thought you were going to ring me when you turned off the A11?'

'Didn't seem much point when we were so close.' She hugged him. 'Hello, darling. This house is incredible.' She put her hands on his shoulders and looked at him. 'And you're finally unwinding. Good.'

And then she spotted Alicia.

'Hello,' she said, smiling.

Jack sighed. 'Mum, this is Alicia Beresford—and her dog, Saffy. Lissy, this is my mum, Anne—and my dad, Mike. My bossy big sister, Cathy; Jimmy you already know; and Lee, my brother.'

'Pleased to meet you,' Alicia said politely.

She was aware of four pairs of eyes staring at her and summing her up, to see if what they'd already heard from Jack and Jimmy was accurate. And then she was smack in the middle of them, being hugged and having her cheek kissed, and Saffy was being fussed over and wagging her tail so hard it was a blur.

This, she thought, was what the house had missed.

Being full of people and chatter and laughter.

And it was somewhere she didn't belong. She'd promised Jack to stay out of the way when his family came—and she'd meant to do it. Except they'd arrived early.

'Um, it was nice to meet you,' she said, edging towards the front door, 'but I'm afraid I'm—'

She didn't get to finish the sentence. 'Oh, don't go on our account,' Anne said with a smile followed by a very pointed look at Jack. 'Stay and have lunch with us.'

Alicia glanced at Jack, whose face was expressionless.

Oh, no. Damned if she stayed, because he didn't want her to; damned if she went, because then she'd be the cause of friction between Jack and his family.

It felt like for ever until he gave her a tiny, tiny nod.

Alicia turned to Anne. 'Thank you. If you're sure.'

'I'll show you round,' Jack said. 'Lissy, do you want to make some coffee?'

In other words, he didn't want her spending any more time than she had to in his family's company. OK. She could deal with this. She smiled brightly. 'Sure.'

Though when they all came back to the kitchen, Jack didn't stand a chance. Alicia was drawn into the conversation, and eventually Anne asked, 'Would you show us the garden?'

Again, she glanced at Jack to check he was OK with it; this time, he looked resigned. She smiled at Anne. 'Sure.'

It felt odd, showing other people round the garden she'd had practically to herself for so long. But then Anne spotted the clematis Alicia had trained up the wall to the vegetable garden. 'Oh, that's *gorgeous*. Can I steal a cutting for my own garden?'

'Sure. I'll sort it out for you before you go back to London,' she promised.

They loved the lake as much as Jack did. And the minute they got back to the house, Mike was at the piano, playing a mix of jazz and classical for them. 'It's a beautiful instrument,' he said approvingly.

Lunch was a hit—especially when Jack informed everyone that the vegetables were from Allingford's garden, grown by Bert and Lissy. Alicia finally started to relax; she was heading for the kitchen on her way back from the loo, planning to make coffee, when she heard voices and stopped by the door.

'So you've finally settled down, then.' Alicia recognised the first voice as Cathy's.

'What do you mean?' Jack asked.

'This place. It's about time, too.'

'No, this is temporary. I live in London. And once the recording studio is up and running and my sabbatical is over, I'll
be going back to London.'

Oh, God. She'd known it. But now it was confirmed. He
wasn't staying.

'What about Alicia?' Cathy asked.

'We're friends.'

Cathy snorted. 'Come off it.'

'Have you seen me touch her today? Kiss her?'

'You don't have to.' Her voice was dry. 'You're practically
ripping her clothes off with your eyes every time you look at
her. Still, at least you've picked a good one this time.'

She could imagine Jack rolling his eyes as he replied, 'I
haven't picked *anything*. Just leave it, Cathy. Don't interfere.
Jimmy's already told her I ought to settle down.'

'And he's right, you should.'

'Not everyone wants marriage and babies, you know,'
Jack pointed out. 'Look, don't interfere. I'm not having a relationship with Lissy. I'm happy as things are and I know
what I'm doing. The recording studio should be up and
running by the end of the summer, and I'm going to rent out
the flats.'

Alicia went cold. No. Surely she'd misheard. *Flats?* As in
both flats? Hers as well as Ted's?

But…

Oh, God. She hadn't been able to face reading the contract—
she'd assumed that the tenancy agreement would be ongoing.
Clearly she'd assumed wrongly. Really wrongly. Because her
tenancy had a time limit.

Just like their affair—because she couldn't be stupid enough
to call it a relationship now.

So of course he wouldn't renew her tenancy. And when their affair was over, she'd have to leave Allingford.

Alicia stood at the door, stricken, wishing she'd never stopped to listen. She knew that Jack had always planned to go back to London; but lately, despite that knowledge, she'd begun to hope that he would stay. Stay with her.

And now she knew for sure.

He was going to leave.

He'd denied that they were anything more than friends.

He was planning to rent out her home to someone else.

And despite the fact that they'd grown so close over the last few weeks, that he'd taken her to paradise and back every night in his arms, Alicia knew now that she'd been fooling herself. He wasn't in love with her. They'd agreed to a no-strings, hot-sex affair. And that was exactly what it had been, in his eyes. The beautiful iris pendant he'd bought her had been just a whim, something that had caught his eye—not a declaration of love. He'd told her he liked her, and now she knew it wasn't an oblique sort of declaration.

OK. She would cope. She'd had to cope with a lot over the previous five years. Even though what she'd learned had cracked her heart in two, she wasn't going to let it show. She'd walk back into the sitting room with her head held high and pretend nothing was wrong.

Thank God she hadn't told Jack that she loved him. She'd be spared his pity, at least.

So even though it hurt like hell, she spent the afternoon being sociable and friendly and smiling and pretending all was well.

When Jack's family had left, she slipped away quietly to take Saffy for a long, long walk on her own.

'Are you OK?' he asked when she finally returned.

'I've got a bit of a headache,' she said. 'Probably because I was up so early this morning.' And it wasn't a complete untruth.

There was an ache. It just happened to be in her heart rather than in her head. 'I think I'll take a couple of paracetamol and have an early night,' she added.

'I could give you a scalp massage,' he offered.

No. Right now she didn't want him to touch her. Not until she'd got her emotions strictly under control and worked out the words to end this relationship-that-wasn't-a-relationship

'I just need some sleep. And I think I really need to be on my own,' she said.

He frowned, but nodded. 'OK. If that's what you want. You know where I am if you need anything.'

'Thanks.' Still keeping her mask of calmness firmly in place, she left the room. And when she was finally in bed—alone— she gave in to the release of hot, silent tears.

This was such a mess.

But better to find out now than to have made a fool of herself, telling Jack she loved him and then seeing the pity in his eyes when he explained that he could never love her back. When he tried to let her down gently. When he explained that she was going to have to leave.

There was only one thing she could salvage from this.

Her pride.

And she'd end this tomorrow.

CHAPTER FOURTEEN

THANK goodness it was Monday, Alicia thought, and she could escape to work. She left early—really early—and sat at her computer in her office, scanning through the websites of the local estate agencies. She needed to find herself somewhere to live. It was going to break her heart to leave Allingford, but she knew she couldn't stay there with Jack any more. Even if she could swallow her pride, it didn't alter the fact that he was going to rent her flat to someone else. That they had no future.

By the time her colleagues had started to arrive at the college, Alicia had found three possible cottages—all reasonably near the college but far enough away from Allingford that she wouldn't keep bumping into Jack. She signed up to several mailing lists, making sure all the details would be sent to the college rather than to her flat.

And all she had to do now was tell Jack it was over.

He was sitting outside her front door when she came home. 'Hey. I called you today. Several times. Didn't you get my voicemails?'

'Sorry. My phone's battery was flat,' she said. It wasn't true, but she was going to have to tell a lot more lies shortly, to save her pride. Might as well get some practice.

He frowned. 'Something's wrong. Tell me.'

I've been stupid enough to fall in love with you, when you're already planning to leave.

The words stuck in her throat.

'Have I done something to hurt you, upset you?'

Not intentionally. But she'd never known pain like this before. Even when she'd lost her father and her brother and the house, she'd managed to keep going. Now…the future was wreathed in shadows.

She swallowed hard. 'I'm having the period from hell.' Another lie. But it was one she was pretty sure would make him keep his distance. The p-word always made men uncomfortable. 'So at the moment I just want to curl up with paracetamol and a hot water bottle.'

'Would a back rub help?'

She'd forgotten his sister was a nurse. Which meant Jack would be one of the rare men who wasn't embarrassed by the subject of menstruation.

'No. I'd just rather be on my own. I feel pretty awful.' That was true. Just not for the same reason.

He gave her a searching look, but at last he nodded. 'If you're sure. Give me a yell if you need anything.'

'I will.' Another fib. Because the one thing she wanted—the one thing he alone could give her—she couldn't have.

Three more days of claiming the period from hell. Three more days of avoiding him. Three more days of looking at details of houses and not being able to find anything that even whispered 'home' to her.

And then, on the Friday, halfway through a tutorial when her students had had enough for the week and weren't remotely concentrating, her mobile phone shrilled.

She glanced at the display: *Simon*.

Oh, help.

She knew what that meant.

She was needed—right now.

'Sorry, I need to take this call. Five minutes—grab a coffee or something,' she told her students, and went out into the corridor. 'Simon?'

'Meg's in labour,' he said.

His parents lived on the south coast and it'd take them a good four hours to get there, even without the rush hour, and Alicia knew that Megan's parents had flown out to Naples two days before. They had a back-up plan that Alicia would look after Jenny while Simon took Meg to hospital. 'I'm on my way,' she reassured him.

'But your students—'

'—are away with the fairies and they'll be delighted to start the weekend early,' she said with a smile. 'Stop panicking. You've done this before and you were brilliant.'

'Thanks, Lissy. You're a gem.'

Her students were indeed delighted to go home early; she drove back to Allingford to drop Saffy at her flat, and Jack was leaning against his car when she came out. 'Hi.'

'Hi. Sorry, can't stay—Meg's gone into labour early and I'm looking after Jenny.'

'Want me to come with you?'

Yes.

She forced herself to ignore the surge of longing. The last thing she needed was to see him with Jenny, have a reminder of what he'd be like as a father and know that he didn't want a child with her. 'No, it's fine.'

'I'll feed Saffy for you. I could bring her over later, if you like,' he offered.

She shook her head. 'Meg has cats and they don't like Saffy.'

'You could bring Jenny back here,' he suggested.

Seeing him with a child at Allingford would be even worse. 'She's better over at Meg and Simon's—her world's about to go through big changes, so being somewhere familiar will be better for her. I'll catch you later.'

He frowned, but let her go. She drove over to Meg's, where Meg was clearly trying to put a brave face on her contractions so as not to frighten Jenny, and Simon looked anxious.

'Go,' she said. 'Jenny and I are going to have a great time.' She produced a box-shaped parcel handbag, wrapped in hologram paper with a big bow on the front. 'Starting here. Because for a special big-sister-to-be on a special day like today, Aunty Lissy's got you a special pressie.'

Jenny's eyes went wide.

'You're wonderful,' Meg whispered, then her face went white as another contraction clearly hit her. 'I think this one's going to come faster than Jenny did.'

'Shoo. Maternity ward. And ring me when I can bring Jenny to meet her little brother or sister,' Alicia directed.

She and Jenny spent a while opening the box together— containing the latest book in the fairy princess set Jenny loved, which Alicia could read to her, a magic wand, a special big-sister tiara, a tiny flower press and a special bug collector. Together, they made a special welcome card for the baby, made cookies, found a ladybird and drew its picture, pressed some flowers, and Alicia painted a butterfly on Jenny's face with face-paints and allowed the little girl to paint her as a tiger.

And that was the point when Alicia realised this was what she wanted. A child to share her life with. A child she could teach about flowers and butterflies and insects; read with, play with, laugh with. A family to love.

For Jenny's sake, she smiled and held back the tears. But it felt as if her biological clock wasn't just ticking, the alarm was clanging and lights were flashing and a siren was going off.

They read more stories together and drew more pictures, and

finally Simon rang. 'Little girl, seven pounds twelve, mum and baby doing well.'

'Fabulous. We're on our way.'

She washed the tiger streaks off her face quickly, strapped Jenny into the car seat and drove to the hospital. As soon as they reached the maternity unit Simon came out of Meg's room to meet them. He picked up his daughter and swung her round. 'Hello, princess! Come and meet Maia.' He looked at Alicia. 'You, too.'

'After Jenny,' she said with a smile.

A few minutes later, Jenny skipped out. 'Aunty Lissy, come and see my little sister.'

Meg looked tired but ecstatic. Simon and Jenny were both excited. And the second he handed her the baby and Alicia smelled that special newborn scent and felt that perfect weight and warmth against her body, her stomach clenched.

She wanted this, too.

Really, *really* wanted it.

A longing like she'd never, ever felt before. Overpowering.

'Are you OK?' Meg asked.

'I'm fine,' Alicia lied. Now was *not* the time to have a heart-to-heart with her best friend. 'But new babies are so beautiful they take your breath away, don't they? She's gorgeous, Meg. Well done.'

'You look a bit broody, the way you're cuddling her,' Simon remarked.

'What, me? Nope. I'm happy being an aunty and god-mother,' she fibbed.

'I'm surprised Jack isn't here,' Simon continued.

'He's looking after Saffy—because I can't bring her to a hospital and your cats would beat her up if I left her at yours. But I'll take a pic to show him.' She smiled at Jenny. 'Hey. Want to be my special photographer?' She'd taught the little girl to use the camera a while back, and, although Jenny still had a habit of cutting off heads and feet and taking pictures of half a flower, she loved doing it. And the camera was light enough for her to handle, Alicia knew.

Jenny beamed and took photographs of Maia in Alicia's arms.

Finally, Jenny was yawning. 'Want me to take her home?' Alicia asked.

'I'll do it,' Simon said with a smile. 'We need to let Meg and our little one get some sleep.' He hugged her. 'Thanks, Lissy. You're a friend in a million.'

'Goes for you lot, too,' she said.

When she returned to Allingford, Jack had clearly been looking after Saffy in his part of the house because her flat was empty. So she was going to have to collect her dog. Steeling herself, she rang the doorbell.

He took a while to answer. And he frowned when he saw her. 'Why didn't you use your key?'

Because it wasn't really hers any more. She evaded the question by asking, 'Is Saffy OK?'

'She's fine. She's sprawled on the sofa, actually.' He leaned over to kiss her but she backed away.

'OK, now I'm really worried. Is Meg all right?'

'Yes. She had a little girl. Maia. They're both doing fine, Simon's as proud as anything and Jenny loves the idea of having a little sister to sing to.'

'So what's wrong?'

'Nothing.'

He coughed. 'I seem to remember having this conversation with you before. Define "nothing".'

'I…' The lump in her throat was so huge that she could barely speak. But this was the right thing to do. Jack didn't love her, and he didn't want what she wanted from life. And time wasn't on her side. The longer she left it to find someone who wanted what she wanted—marriage and babies with *her*—the longer it would take her to fall pregnant. She couldn't afford to wait around for Jack and hope he changed his mind.

'You know what we said? About when it's over, letting the other one down gently?' she whispered.

His eyes widened. 'Over? You're telling me it's over?'

She nodded. 'If you could just get Saffy for me. I'm sorry, Jack. I hope you find what you're looking for.'

If only it could've been her.

Jack was too shocked to do anything other than fetch the dog. Although he was used to dealing with the unexpected, handled crises with aplomb, for the second time in his life he was completely thrown.

'Lissy, we need to talk about this,' he said when he came back to the door, Saffy by his side.

'Nothing to talk about. I'm sorry.'

She clicked her tongue, the Labrador trotted out obediently, and then they walked away.

He couldn't take this in.

It was over.

And she wasn't even giving him the chance to find out what had gone wrong.

He could go after her, but he knew she'd clam up. He needed to regroup. Work out a strategy. And then make her tell him what was in her head.

The house felt empty and chilly without her. His bed was worse, and he spent a sleepless night, unable to settle. He'd just downed a mug of strong coffee the next morning and was trying to work out how to tackle Alicia when his phone rang.

'Jack? It's Keely. Will's been taken into hospital.'

Keely was his assistant at work. Will had taken over from him during his sabbatical.

'Is he all right? What happened?'

'Not sure. They're doing tests. But he's worrying about—'

'Work?' Jack cut in gently. 'Tell him from me, there's nothing to worry about. I'm on my way. Which hospital?'

'London City General.'

'OK. I'll be there soon. And everything's going to be fine.'

Despite the fact that it was still ridiculously early, especially for a Saturday morning, Alicia's car wasn't outside. Which meant she was doing major avoidance tactics. He took one of his business cards from his wallet and scribbled a note on the back. 'Called to London. Not sure how long will be away. Back soon. Need to talk.' He posted it through her letterbox, and headed to London.

It took until Thursday to sort everything out—to arrange a replacement for Will, to hand-hold Will's new replacement, Becky, through the first morning until she felt confident enough to handle things on her own with a hotline to Jack if she needed him. All the way back to Norfolk, he was wondering how to deal with Alicia—how to get her to tell him the truth about why she'd dumped him.

Because he was beginning to realise now that this wasn't what he wanted. No-strings hot sex wasn't enough.

He wanted *her*.

The second he pulled into the drive, he registered that another car was parked outside Alicia's flat. A car he didn't know. It was too new and too expensive to belong to Grace's boyfriend; he was pretty sure it didn't belong to Meg or Simon. So who…?

Jealousy flickered in his gut and he leaned on her doorbell.

As soon as she opened the door, without giving her a chance to say a word, he said, 'Lissy, we need to talk.'

'Now's not a good time.'

And as if in response to the wariness in her voice, a man walked out of her kitchen. 'Everything all right, Lissy?'

His first thought was relief that the man wasn't Gavin.

His second was wondering what that man was doing with *his* woman.

'Everything's fine, Derek. My landlord.' She looked at Jack. 'And he's?'

'My...' she paused '...friend.'

It'd better mean *just* friend and not lover, Jack thought. He had to make a conscious effort not to bunch his fists or grab the bloke and bundle him out.

'Perhaps we can discuss things tomorrow when I get back from the college.'

In other words, she didn't want a scene in front of her new man.

At least, he thought, she'd dumped him before she'd started seeing someone else.

'Of course,' he said, as coolly as he could manage, and turned away.

His mood got worse after another night with not enough sleep. He had a stand-up row with the builders, the following afternoon, and only Grace's arrival stopped it turning really nasty.

'Ignore him,' Grace said to the builder. 'Lack of cake.' She pushed him into the kitchen. 'What was that all about?'

'Nothing.'

She raised an eyebrow. 'You've had a fight with Lissy, haven't you?'

'Is that what she said?'

'No. But she's in as bad a mood as you are.'

'She dumped me.'

Grace frowned, made instant coffee and put the mug in front of him. 'Since when?'

'Last week. She's seeing someone else.'

'What?' Grace scoffed. 'No way. Who?'

'Some guy called Derek.'

'Hang on.' Grace grabbed her mobile phone and punched in

a number. 'Meg? It's Grace. Do you know someone called Derek—someone who knows Lissy? Uh-huh, uh-huh. Got it. Thanks. See ya.' She put the phone down. 'He's the bursar at the college.'

He relaxed. 'So it's work.'

Grace squirmed. 'Um, no. According to Meg, he's had the hots for Lissy for ages—he's asked her out a couple of times and she's always turned him down.' She frowned. 'What did you do?'

'I have no idea.'

'I thought you liked her.'

'I do.' More than liked. 'I don't know what's going on in her head. She's been acting weird ever since my family came over. But I have no idea why—my family's fantastic. My sister's a bit bossy but her heart's in the right place, and they all know when to back off and give me space. They liked her. And I thought she liked them.' He shook his head. 'I don't get it.'

'Have you actually asked her why she dumped you?' she asked.

'She won't talk to me.'

'Then do the caveman thing.'

Jack was completely lost. 'What?'

'*Duh*. Caveman,' Grace said, rolling her eyes. 'Carry her off to bed. And when you've worked your magic so she can't think any more, ask her how she feels. You'll get the truth then.'

He blinked. 'Grace, you're eighteen. How come you…?'

'Know so much about sex?' She grinned. 'When you're a barmaid, people talk to you. Spill their hearts out over their pint. So I have a lot of wisdom from other people.'

'Haul her off to bed.' He liked that idea.

'Oh, and make sure you have chocolate supplies. Sex and chocolate. It's an unbeatable combination.'

He laughed. 'I never thought I'd be taking advice on my love life from someone ten years younger than me.'

'Don't knock it.'

'Will it work?'

Grace spread her hands. 'What have you got to lose?'

Lissy, he thought. I stand to lose Lissy.

If I haven't lost her already.

CHAPTER FIFTEEN

JACK bought chocolate. Posh chocolate from the farm shop in the village, made by a local chocolatier. And he stashed the box in his bedside table next to the condoms.

This had better work.

Because he wanted Alicia back. In his bed, in his life—and in his heart.

She'd promised to come and see him after lectures. And even listening to music or playing the piano or strumming the guitar he'd brought back from London didn't help. He was too on edge. In the end, he resorted to pacing through the house. And he was feeling more and more like a caged tiger when she finally rang the doorbell.

Why didn't she use her key?

He yanked the door open and scowled at her.

'Hello to you, too. So what did you want to talk about?' she asked.

'A few things. Come in.' He ushered her into the kitchen. 'Why are you seeing that guy?'

'What guy?'

'Derek.' He faced her, unsmiling. 'He looks ten years older than you.'

'He isn't. Actually, he's two years older than me.'

'Then he isn't ageing well. He combs his hair over the thin patch and he dresses as if he's fifty.'

She frowned. 'What's that got to do with anything?'

'Answer the question. Why are you seeing him?'

'Because…' She stopped short. 'I don't have to explain myself to you.'

'Yes, you do. You dumped me.'

'We weren't having a relationship,' she reminded him.

Oh, yes, they were. 'I need to know. And I can't read your mind, Lissy. Tell me.'

She folded her arms. 'All right. Seeing Maia when she was less than an hour old made me realise something. That I want more than you can offer me. I don't want just sex.'

'It isn't "just sex". It's good sex. It's *fantastic* sex,' he corrected.

'But it's still sex. You've said all along you don't want marriage and babies.'

He still didn't see where this was going. 'So did you.'

'But I do now. It was like a switch was turned, Jack. And everywhere I look, I see babies. I see couples. I see people who are settled. And look at me. I'm thirty-four years old. I have a rented flat and a dead-end job.'

He frowned. 'I thought you loved your job.'

'I did. I *do*. But the prospects of promotion at the college are practically nil. The only way I'll get any further up the scale is if I teach somewhere else.' She dragged in a breath. 'And this isn't my home any more. You're right, it's time I faced up to it and stopped trying to live in the past. I need to move on. Find somewhere else. Find some*one* else.'

'Someone who'll give you babies.'

'Yes. I'm thirty-four, Jack. I don't have time to wait around and hope that Mr Right will come along. I need to find him. While I'm still fertile enough to get pregnant relatively easily.'

He went very still. 'You could have babies with me.'

'No, I couldn't. It isn't what you want.'

He felt his eyes narrow. 'How do you know what I want?'

'Because you told me. You've been married before. You got taken to the cleaners. You don't trust anyone. And—'

Caveman it was going to be. He didn't wait for her to finish. He simply hauled her into his arms and jammed his mouth over hers. Kissed her until she started to respond. And then he simply picked her up in his arms and carried her up to his bed.

Where she belonged.

'Jack, we—' she began when he laid her on the bed.

'No talking.' Just to make the point, he kissed her again. And when she started kissing him back, he made short work of removing their clothes.

She shouldn't be doing this.

They shouldn't be doing this.

But, Lord help her, his touch was irresistible. The way his fingers skimmed her curves, caressing her, stoking her desire until she was practically begging him to take her. The way his mouth found all her sensitive points and nipped and licked and sucked until she was quivering. The way he nudged between her thighs and paused at her entrance, waiting for her.

'Yes,' she hissed, and he pushed deep inside her.

He was kissing her again, deep and hard and wet and hot. Every thrust mirrored by the movement of his tongue. And his hands were lifting her slightly, changing the angle so he could push deeper, deeper, filling her so completely and so pleasurably.

Her climax was swift and shocking.

And her head was still spinning when he eased out of her.

'Is Derek going to be able to offer you that?' he demanded. 'Does he make your blood heat like that every time he kisses you?'

No, of course he didn't. Actually, Alicia had avoided Derek's kisses—because it felt wrong, wrong, wrong when she wanted Jack so badly.

'Your silence proves my point. Because he doesn't, does he?'

No. But that wasn't what all this was about. Alicia glared at him. 'But he can offer me something else,' she said. 'He's ready to settle down. He wants marriage. Babies. And you don't.' She wriggled out of his arms and pulled on her knickers and T-shirt before bundling the rest of her clothes in her arms and stomping over to the door. 'I admit, the sex is good. More than good. But I want *more* than sex, Jack. Something you can't give me.' She faced him, unsmiling. 'And we're not doing this again.'

'Lissy…'

His only answer was the slam of his bedroom door. And even though he didn't bother waiting to put any clothes on and ran straight out after her, she was faster because she knew the house better. The front door slammed even harder before he could get to it. And he knew she'd have her own door double-locked before he could get there.

This wasn't over.

But maybe caveman was the wrong way.

'Right. Sit.'

Grace blinked. 'Blimey. You definitely got out of the wrong side of the bed this morning.'

Jack rolled his eyes. 'Tell me about it. And it's the last time I'm taking advice from you.'

'Adv…?' Grace winced. 'Oh. You and Lissy still haven't—'

'Caveman doesn't work,' Jack cut in. 'So we're going to do this my way, now. You're setting her up on a blind date.'

'I'm doing *what*?'

'You heard,' Jack said. 'You're going to tell her you've found the perfect man for her. Someone who wants the same kind of thing she wants. And you're setting her up on a blind date.'

Grace shook her head. 'She won't go for it. She'll say she's too old for all the men I know from college.'

'All right. If you won't help me, then I'll ask Meg—'

'Who has a tiny baby and isn't getting much sleep so wouldn't remember to get the day or the time right,' Grace cut in archly.

He scowled. 'I need to know that Lissy's going to show up at a certain place and a certain time. So if a blind date isn't going to work…how about a girly night with you and Meg?'

'Nope. Meg's not going to leave her baby for that long.'

Jack raked a hand through his hair. 'For goodness' sake, will you stop putting obstacles in my way?'

'I'm not. But I don't know if Lissy's ready for something like this. Although she's just been moping around the house, and it would be good for her to get out. This needs to be convincing…' She shrugged. 'OK. Not a girly night. We could do a quick—and I mean *really* quick—drink, so Meg can get outside the four walls. Except…you know Lissy. She'll suggest picking us all up.'

He shook his head. 'She has to arrive on her own.'

Grace sighed. 'Back to your blind date idea, then. And you're right, you'll have to involve Meg to make it believable. Tell me the details and I'll make sure Meg does it by phone so I can prompt her if I have to.'

'Thank you. And I'm going back to London.'

'Why?'

'Absence makes the heart grow fonder.' Jack scribbled details down on a pad and ripped off the top sheet. 'Here you go.'

'So where are you taking her?'

'Not important.'

Grace rolled her eyes. 'Of course it is. She's going to want to know how to dress.'

'Dressy.'

'How dressy?'

'Just dressy.'

Grace folded her arms. 'Do you want me to do this, or not?'

So he told her.

'They don't open on Wednesdays.'

'They will for me.'

Grace whistled. 'How did you swing that?'

He grinned. 'I'm not telling you all my trade secrets.'

She looked thoughtful. 'You know, I've always wanted to go there…'

He sighed. 'All right. I'll book a table for you and your boyfriend and the bill's on me.'

'And Meg and Simon?'

'I can't see you double-dating, but, yes. Meg, too. I owe you both, if you can get Lissy to meet me there—except I don't want her to know it's me.'

'Why?'

'Because I'm afraid she won't turn up,' Jack said quietly.

'Leave it to me and I'll get it set up. But, this time, *don't* mess it up.' Her smile faded. 'And if you hurt Lissy, you've got me to deal with.'

'I'm not going to hurt her,' Jack said softly. 'I've just woken up and realised what I want for the rest of my life.'

'All right,' Grace said. 'I need to go and see Meg.'

'Thanks, Meg, but I don't want to go on a blind date,' Alicia said.

'It'll cheer you up a bit.'

'I don't *need* cheering up,' Alicia lied.

Meg sighed. 'Look, I'm sorry things didn't work out with Jack. But you have to move on. If you're serious about meeting someone and getting married and starting a family…'

'I wish I hadn't told you about that now,' Alicia muttered.

'Who else are you going to tell except your best friend? Listen, I know this guy who'd be just perfect for you. He's gorgeous, he's got a sense of humour, he has all his own hair and his own teeth.'

'So why's he unattached, then?' Alicia asked suspiciously.

There was a pause. 'Because…I dunno. He works too hard. Doesn't have a social life. And he's reached the point where he's realised that he wants to settle down. You'd be good for each other, Lissy. And if nothing else it'll fill some time and stop you thinking about Jack Goddard for a few seconds.'

'Thanks, but no, thanks.'

'Lissy, just give it a go. It'll be fun.'

Alicia doubted it, but at the same time she didn't want to hurt her best friend's feelings. 'So who is this man?'

'A business contact of Simon's.'

'And his name?'

'Um…'

'Meg, if you don't even know his name, how on earth can you set me up on a date with him?'

'I'm sleep-deprived, hormonal and breast-feeding,' Meg retorted. 'What about last week, when I put the box of teabags in the fridge and the milk in the cupboard?'

Alicia laughed. 'OK, point taken.' And maybe Meg was right. Maybe a night out with someone she didn't even know would turn out to be fun. 'Tell me where and when.'

'Wednesday night. He'll send a taxi to bring you to a restaurant.'

'Why?'

'Because…he's working on this project and won't have time to pick you up himself.'

'This smells a bit fishy.'

'Maia needs feeding.'

'You can talk and breast-feed at the same time,' Alicia said, 'and you did it with Jenny as well, so don't try to con me.'

'The man's a workaholic and so are you. You'll have a fine time. The taxi will take you to the restaurant and he'll meet you there.'

'Which restaurant?'

'I forgot. But it does wonderful *crème brûlée*, I remember that much. With rhubarb and ginger compote. Order that.'

'You remember the menu but not the restaurant name.' This was sounding more and more suspicious.

'I'm rubbish with names at the moment, Lissy. I'm trying to do something nice for my best friend.'

And even though it was against her better judgement, Alicia knew Meg meant well. She'd go, but she'd quietly reverse the last three digits of her phone number when the guy asked for it. 'All right.'

'Good. And let Grace do your hair.'

'I can do my own hair.'

'Not in a scrunchie, Lissy. Your hair's too pretty to be mauled about like that.'

Alicia judged it wise not to have that argument. 'Wednesday. What time?'

'Seven. Just go and have some fun, for a change.'

Without Jack, Alicia wasn't sure that anything would be fun. But Meg had a point. It would kill some time. And stop her thinking about Jack for all of three seconds. 'OK.'

By the time Wednesday came around, Jack still hadn't returned from London. Alicia tried to put him out of her mind and concentrate on her blind date.

But when the taxi arrived at its destination, she stared in surprise. Yes, it was a foodie pub. And she knew the food was fabulous because it was one of Meg's favourites. But it wasn't usually open on Wednesday nights. Meg must've got it wrong…but, then again, if Meg had got the date wrong, why had the taxi turned up? 'There must be some mistake,' she said.

'These were my instructions, Ms Beresford,' the driver said.

She frowned. 'Would you mind waiting a moment, please? Because it doesn't look open to me—and if it's not, I'll need to get back home. I don't want to be stranded here in the middle of nowhere.'

'Of course,' the driver said.

But the second he opened the car door for her, the front door of the restaurant opened and the *maître d'* stood there, waiting to greet her.

'I think you're going to be OK, love. Special occasion, is it?' the taxi driver asked knowingly.

'Something like that,' she said lightly. But, actually, it was the weirdest blind date she'd ever been on. Who on earth *was* this friend of Simon's?

The *maître d'* welcomed her and settled her in the restaurant with a glass of champagne. Most of the tables had been stacked away; there was just one table in the middle of the room. A table set with a white starched linen tablecloth, silver and a candelabrum. Soft jazz piano was playing in the background.

Whoever Meg's mystery man was, he either had excellent connections or he was very persuasive, to get this place to open for him alone.

And then a voice she recognised said softly, 'Hello, Lissy.'

She stared as Jack sat opposite her. 'What are you doing here?'

He smiled. 'Got a hot date.'

With her? She continued to stare at him. 'No, this can't be right.'

'Who did you think it'd be?' he asked mildly.

'I don't know. But not you. You're in London.'

'Was,' he said drily. 'Will—who took over from me while I was on sabbatical—ended up in hospital. And I had to take over the reins until Becky, Will's number two, could take over from me.'

'Is he all right?'

'He'll be fine, but he needs to convalesce for the next few

months. It was a heart attack. Which, at the age of thirty, isn't good. It gave me pause for thought about my lifestyle in London.'

'But you're going back there. It's where you belong.'

'Hmm. We'll discuss this later. So now we've established I'm not in London, why else wouldn't it be me?'

'Because you don't want to marry me or have babies with me.'

'What makes you think that?'

'Because I overheard you talking to your sister. She was telling you that you should settle down, and you said that not everyone wants marriage and babies.

He shrugged. 'I have that conversation with her every single week.'

'You said you were going back to London—and you were going to rent out the flats. As in plural. I *heard* you. Ted's flat—and mine.'

'At least now I know why you suddenly went cold on me.' He shook his head. 'I should've pushed you a lot harder to tell me what was in your head and we could have saved ourselves so much misery. Yes, I will want to go back to London for some of the time—but I'm also planning to spend a lot of time here. And, yes, I probably will rent out the flats, because otherwise they're just going to be empty.'

'So you're throwing me out of Allingford.'

'No. Your flat's going to be empty because I want you to move in with me properly.' He paused. 'The thing is, Lissy, I fell in love with a house. And a lake. And a dog. And this slightly scruffy, slightly posh woman that came right along with them.' He gave her one of those quirky smiles that always made her pulse beat a bit faster. 'I realised I loved you, the day we went to Norwich. When I found myself buying jewellery for you—I never, ever buy jewellery for anyone I date. And I was hideously jealous of Gavin.'

'Of Gavin? That's crazy. It was over a long time ago.'

'On your part, maybe. But I saw the way he looked at you. I tried to kid myself that I was only jealous because it reminded me of what happened with Erica, but it wasn't that at all. I hated the idea of him being anywhere near you. And it drove me crazy when I saw you with Derek.'

She shook her head. 'Derek hasn't even held my hand.'

'Good. Keep it that way.' His eyes were very intense. 'Anyway. Just so you know. I love you.'

'You love me,' she repeated.

'And I don't say those words lightly.' His eyes were very intense.

She stared at him, hardly able to believe what she was hearing. 'You love me.'

'Uh-huh. And, yes, Meg and Grace both know this. They both know that I want to—' He stopped short. 'Later. Now, can you try a different pronoun and object in your next sentence? You can keep the verb.'

Mischief made her say, 'Saffy loves chicken.'

He groaned. 'That wasn't what I meant.'

She laughed. 'OK. I love you, too.'

'Good.' He paused. 'So when did you know?'

'In Norwich. When you were trying to protect me from Gavin. I love your zest for life. The fact you're so sure of yourself, that you know what you want and you go for it—but at the same time you try not to hurt others. I love the way you don't mind when my dog covers you in mud. I love the way you—I love the way you make me feel complete, when we make love.'

'Do you, now?' he said thoughtfully. He made a signal, and the waiter came over with a silver salver, placed it in front of Alicia, and then discreetly withdrew.

A minute passed, and Jack asked, 'Aren't you going to open it?'

'What about yours?'

'Later.'

She frowned.

He rolled his eyes. 'OK. I'll take the lid off for you.' He stood next to her and whisked the silver dome aside.

Underneath was the most beautiful arrangement of blue flowers. Natural blue, she noticed, not dyed blue. Delphiniums and irises, set off by delicate white gypsophilium. And nestling in the middle was a small box, tied with pale blue pearlescent ribbon. The label said simply, 'Alicia.'

She looked at the box, and then at him.

'Open it,' he said softly.

She untied the ribbon. Gently flipped up the lid of the box. And as the plain solitaire diamond glittered in the candlelight tears pricked her eyes. 'It's beautiful.'

He dropped to one knee beside her and took her left hand. Pressed the lightest, gentlest kiss on her ring finger. 'I love you, Alicia Beresford. My life isn't right without you in the middle of it. And I want it all. Marriage, children, a life we make together. Will you marry me?'

'Just so you know,' she said, 'my answer has nothing to do with the house.'

'Of course not. You're no gold-digger.'

'And there are no conditions.'

'We're not talking gardens tonight,' he agreed.

'But…' she tipped her head on one side '…I'd quite like to keep the hot sex part.'

His smile turned positively wolfish. 'Absolutely. And although this is a very private engagement party, I'll wait until we get home before I ravish you.'

'That's a promise?'

'Answer my question first, and then I'll tell you.'

She smiled. 'Yes, I'll marry you.'

His kiss was slow and sweet and full of promise.

'Good,' he said softly. 'Because I'll tell you now, I'll love you for the rest of my days. And I always keep my promises.'

'I know. You're a man of honour.'

He took the ring from the box and slid it onto her finger. 'A perfect fit. Just like we are—you, me, Saffy, the house.' He smiled at her. 'And, in the future, our children.'

Celebrate 100 years of pure reading pleasure with Mills & Boon®

To mark our centenary, each month we're publishing a special 100th Birthday Edition. These celebratory editions are packed with extra features and include a FREE bonus story.

Now that's worth celebrating!

4th January 2008

The Vanishing Viscountess by Diane Gaston
With FREE story The Mysterious Miss M
This award-winning tale of the Regency Underworld launched Diane Gaston's writing career.

1st February 2008

Cattle Rancher, Secret Son by Margaret Way
With FREE story His Heiress Wife
Margaret Way excels at rugged Outback heroes…

15th February 2008

Raintree: Inferno by Linda Howard
With FREE story Loving Evangeline
A double dose of Linda Howard's heady mix of passion and adventure.

Don't miss out! From February you'll have the chance to enter our fabulous monthly prize draw. See special 100th Birthday Editions for details.

www.millsandboon.co.uk